CRAIG HALLORAN

DON'T FORGET YOUR FREE BOOKS

Join my newsletter and receive three magnificent stories from my bestselling series for FREE!

Not to mention that you'll have direct access to my collection of over 80 books, including audiobooks and boxsets. FREE and .99 cents giveaways galore!

Sign up here!

WWW.DRAGONWARSBOOKS.COM

Finally, please leave a review of Monarch Madness-Book 6 when you finish. I've typed my fingers to the bone writing it and your reviews are a huge help!

MONARCH MADNESS REVIEW LINK

Dragon Wars: Monarch Madness - Book 6

By Craig Halloran

★★★★

Publisher's Note

This book is a work of fiction. Names, characters, places, and incidents either are the product of the author's imagination or are used fictitiously, and any resemblance to actual persons, living or dead, events, or locales is entirely coincidental.

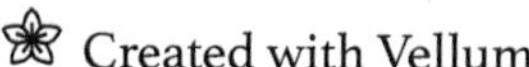 Created with Vellum

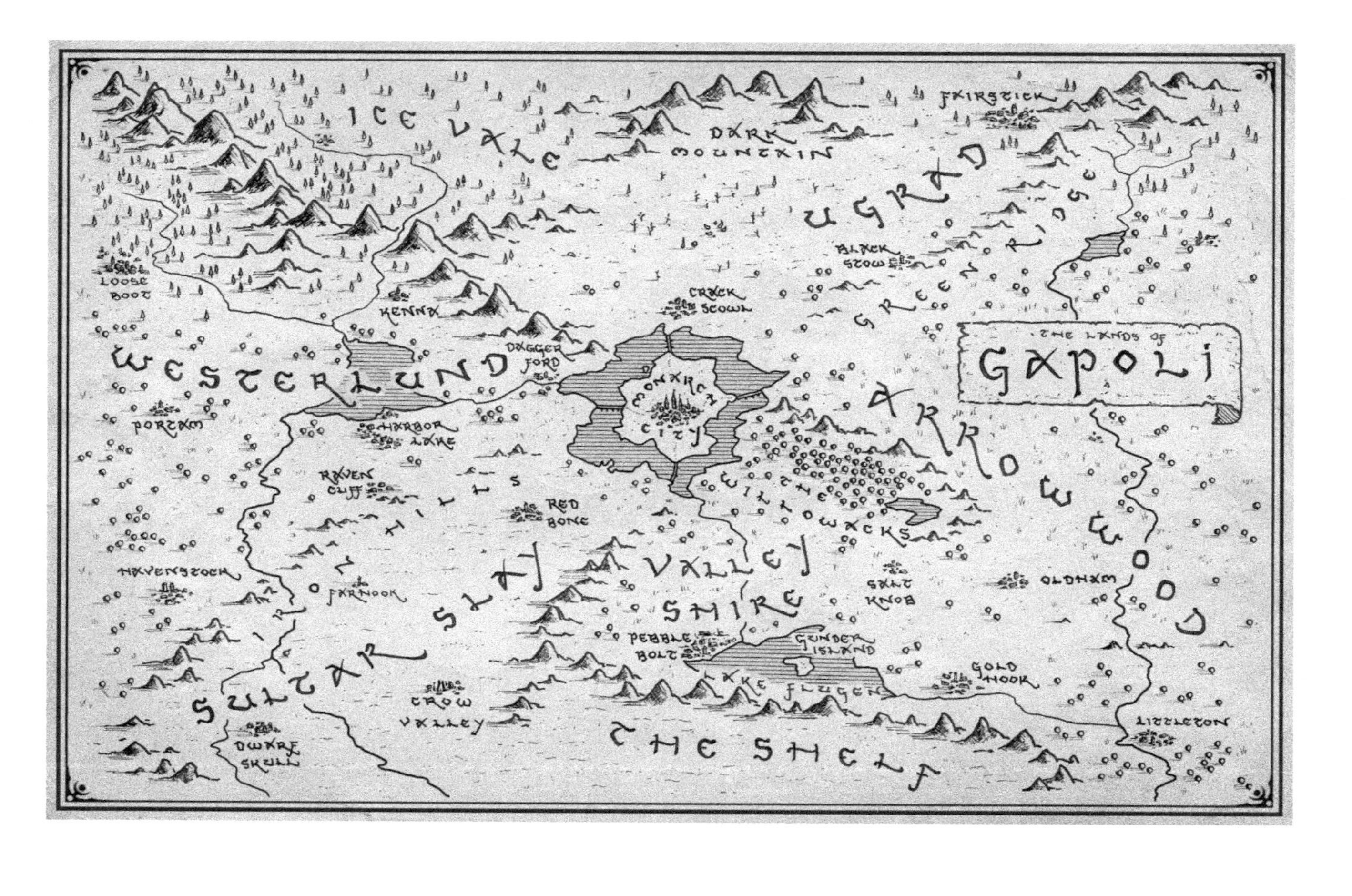

ICE VALE
DARK MOUNTAIN
FAIRSTICK
UGRAD
GREEN RIDGE
BLACK SCOWL
CRACK SCOWL
THE LANDS OF GAPOLI
WESTERLUND
LOOSE BOOT
KENNA
DAGGER FORD
MONARCH CITY
ARROW WOOD
PORTAM
HARBOR LAKE
RAVEN CLIFF
THE HILLS
RED BONE
THE WILLOWACKS
SALT KNOB
OLDHAM
HAVENSTOCK
FARNOOK
SULTAR SLAY VALLEY
SHIRE
PEBBLE BOLT
GUNDER ISLAND
LAKE FLUGEN
GOLD HOOK
CROW VALLEY
DWARF SKULL
THE SHELF
LITTLETON

MONARCH CITY

Grey Cloak paced through the cozy apartment that Crane had set up for Zora, Dyphestive, and himself. Coffee was brewing on the stove, and Dyphestive sat half-filling the sofa, admiring his statue of Codd. Thanadiliditis, the hermit, sat on the other side of the sofa, stroking Streak's back, who was nestled in his lap. Leena, a monk from the Ministry of Hoods, was squeezed in between the two men, her typical intense look in her eyes.

Jakoby sat at a small table. The dark-skinned warrior wore an easygoing expression as he sipped a mug of coffee.

"Yonders. Of all things, they have yonders everywhere. It's going to be impossible to get Codd's shield out of Monarch Castle unseen," Grey Cloak said. He'd been muttering to himself ever since he departed the castle, trying to think of ideas for how he could rescue Zora from

Irsk Monco, the leader of the Dark Addler. "It's no wonder *you* wanted me to see for myself." He looked dead at Jakoby.

Jakoby, the former Monarch Knight, set his mug aside. "It's one of those things that you need to see for yourself. You have to understand what you're up against. Yes, you have the yonders, not to mention the Honor Guard as well. That makes the very notion of stealing Codd's shield unthinkable."

Grey Cloak wrung his hands. "It would be doable if it weren't for the yonders. Flying eyeballs with wings? Who comes up with these things?"

"The castle's enchanters," Jakoby replied. "They're weird people. At least that's what people say. I only saw the yonders a few times when I was a knight. Spooky."

Grey Cloak stopped pacing and crossed his arms. "Well, that helps a lot. Thank you. Does anyone else have any useful information that they would like to share? How about you, hermit? You're awfully quiet. Any ideas?"

Than combed his scaly fingers through his stringy red-streaked white hair. "If I did, I would have shared them. I do think you're on the right track to infiltrate the castle, but you'll be on your own once you're in there. We can't help, seeing as they're hunting for us as we speak."

Grey Cloak watched Dyphestive intently playing with his toy. Grey Cloak snatched it out of his hand and set it on the mantel above the small fireplace. "Will you pay attention?"

Dyphestive frowned. "I was."

"No, you weren't. You've been obsessed with that statue ever since you brought it home."

"But the detail."

"I don't want to hear about the details. I want to hear ideas about how to help Zora." Grey Cloak's nostrils flared. He was losing his composure, and he knew it. It wasn't like him, but he'd never felt pressure like this. He gathered his thoughts. "Let's hash this out again, shall we?"

Jakoby leaned over his coffee. "Hash it out as many times as you want. You never know what might come to mind. I'll tell you what. Let me hash it out, and you listen. It might spark an idea."

Grey Cloak nodded.

Jakoby pushed a chair out with his foot. "Have a seat and listen." Grey Cloak obeyed, and Jakoby continued. "We all know Irsk Mondo. Part elf, part goblin. The leader of the Dark Addler. He came after you"—he pointed to Grey Cloak and Dyphestive—"because you freed the Gunthy children and us in the process. Now he's taken Zora hostage, and he wants ten thousand gold chips and your dragon or the shield of Codd in exchange for her. Correct?"

"Correct. I don't see how this is helping," Grey Cloak added.

Jakoby drew himself up in a noble manner. "Keep listening. I'm not at the end yet."

Grey Cloak nodded.

"Codd's shield is guarded in the very heart of Monarch Castle. The two of you have seen it, and I've seen it. Twelve Honor Guards are stationed in Codd's crypt *and* who knows how many yonders? It sounds like the yonders focus more on the castle tours, but I could be wrong.

"We have two choices. First, we can steal Codd's shield and exchange it for Zora. That sounds impossible. Or we can shell out ten thousand chips and your dragon." Jakoby eyed Streak, who was still lounging comfortably on Than's lap. "But that is the same as exchanging one friend for another. You won't win anything by doing that." He eyed Grey Cloak. "Does that help?"

"No, that doesn't help. All you did was hash out what we've already been talking about for over an hour." Grey Cloak sighed, leaned his elbows on his knees, and rubbed his temples. "It's making my skull ache."

"Just because Irsk Monco gave you two options doesn't mean those are the only two options you have," Jakoby said.

Grey Cloak lifted his head. "What do you mean?"

"He gave you parameters. You need to think outside of those parameters. That's what they teach the Monarch Knights. Change the game. You've shown a knack for that by infiltrating the castle. Build on it. Use your creativity,"

Jakoby said. "There is more than one way to skin a dragon, we say." He glanced at Streak, who turned his head toward him and flicked out his tongue. "No offense."

"I'm trying, but I've hit a wall. I have a way into the castle, but I don't have a way out with the shield. Don't any of you have anything creative?"

"I'm fine with a sword, but I'm not the most creative thinker," Jakoby said as he patted his pommel. "I prefer to let my steel do the heavy thinking for me when I'm in a bind. Irsk Monco and his brood are evil. I prefer to kill the likes of him outright."

"I would like to do so myself." Grey Cloak envisioned the last time he saw Zora's pretty face. She was in the rough hands of the Iron Devils. The robed men's iron masks were fashioned with sinister expressions, and she was scared for her life. Her voice had cracked when she spoke. He'd never heard Zora like that before. "But we don't know where she is. Should we go after them? We could try to trail my contact, Orpah."

"I don't think you have enough swords to take on the Dark Addler," Than said. He leaned forward with Streak resting on his shoulder like a baby. "I'm all for looking evil dead in the eye and destroying it. People like that don't often change their ways. I believe in redemption, but I believe in killing, too, as a last resort, especially when it's them or you. Don't blink."

"Should we try to find Zora, then?" Grey Cloak asked.

"Let us handle that." Than scratched Streak between the small horns on his head. "I think your plan to infiltrate the castle is a sound one. You might find the crease you need."

Dyphestive stood up, walked over to the mantel, grabbed his figurine, and sat back down. His eyes were intent on every detail of Codd's suit of armor. He was fascinated with it.

Grey Cloak's jaw tightened. *I have one hundred ideas racing through my mind, and my brother wants to play with a toy.* He stood up and headed for the exit.

"Where are you going?" Jakoby asked.

He opened the door. "To take a walk and clear my mind." He slammed the door behind him.

2

———

Grey Cloak sauntered down the stone-paved streets of Monarch City, deep in thought. On the one hand, Jakoby had opened a door for him. On the other hand, it didn't make his task any easier, and Zora's life was on the line.

Ten thousand chips and my dragon. Preposterous. Irsk knows I can't do that. Is he toying with me?

It might be a game to the leader of the Dark Addler, but Grey Cloak had cost the man a lot of money, and thieves didn't like that. He knew because he wouldn't like it either. Irsk wanted his money back or something of equal or greater value. So far, that was Zora.

I could steal the money from someone else. Perhaps I could pilfer a money lender's vault.

He passed by one such institution as he thought about

it. The money lenders had vaults spread throughout the city. The stone buildings were under heavy guard. Two orc sentries stood at the entry to the vault he was passing. Their heavy stares locked right on him. He averted his eyes and moved on.

Grey Cloak's tummy rumbled. He hadn't eaten much, and it was catching up to him. Since he was near the Tavern Dwellers Inn, he decided to stop in, as an idea had crossed his mind. It was early evening, past sunset, and the tavern was at full capacity. He waved to Aham the Watchful, a slink with a gelatinous body and tentacles with many eyes.

Aham wobbled across the floor toward him, his tentacles waving. "Have you come to work? Busy night," he said in a bubbly voice. "We need all hands on deck."

"Sorry, I have other business, Aham. If you'll excuse me." He pushed by his employer and slid toward the back.

He nearly bumped into Teena, a cute waitress with bouncy curls, on his way through. She had a full serving tray on her shoulder.

"Glad you're here. I could use some help."

He patted her on the hip. "Sorry, not tonight."

"What?" she asked with disapproval. "Ah, I knew you wouldn't last."

He pushed to the back corner of the tavern and caught the eye of Irsk's envoy, Orpah.

The husky orcen woman, who packed on the makeup

and squeezed into tight, gaudy clothing, waved him over with her flabby arms. Her valuable bracelets jingled along her meaty wrists. Orpah swept her hair from her eyes when he sat down. "Would you like something to eat, cute one? You look hungry."

The table was covered in what could have been every meal from the menu. Even though he was hungry, he didn't want to touch any of it. It was all half-eaten.

"No, thank you. I want you to tell Irsk that I need more time. Two days."

Orpah belched and tapped her chest. "Excuse me." She dabbed gravy from her chin and picked up a ham bone. "That's going to be as impossible as your mission."

"But I can't do this," he pleaded. "It's impossible. Please ask for more time. I need it. I'll come up with the money somehow."

She gave him a sympathetic look, bit into her ham bone, and with her mouth full, she said, "Oh, you poor dear. I really feel for you, but he won't change his mind. If you don't deliver, then your adorable little friend will be gone in one way or another." She lifted a greasy finger. "But you can learn from this, can't you?"

"Learn what?"

"To keep your nose out of other people's business." She snorted as she ate. "Now, run along. I'm expecting someone with a situation very similar to yours, but I don't think they'll make it either. See you in two and a half days." She winked. "I hope you have what we want."

He stormed away from the table and hurried outside. He knew asking for more time was a long shot, but it was worth a try. Besides, he had an ulterior motive.

Let them see my desperation. Perhaps they'll lower their guard.

He walked the streets for the longest time, trying to visualize how he could pull off the heist. He thought inside and outside the box.

I have to figure it out. It's like Jakoby said. There's more than one way to skin a dragon. And if it can be done, I can do it.

He felt a chill and looked sideways. He stopped. Crammed in what he knew used to be an alley between two stores was a tall, slender wooden building with a large red door. The sign over the door read: Batram's Bartery and Arcania.

Grey Cloak was pretty sure Batram was mad at him about the last time they met. He turned his foot toward the strange store. *I'll take my chances.*

3

"May I see that statue?" Jakoby asked Dyphestive.

Dyphestive leaned over Leena and slid the figurine of Codd to the end of the table. "Be careful with it."

"Oh, I will be," Jakoby said as he picked it up and gave it a close examination. "How much did you pay for this?"

"Five gold chips."

"Really? That's a lot of money, but I have to admit that the detail is remarkable." He slid the small sword out of the scabbard. "Hah!"

"Be careful with it, will you?" Dyphestive started to go for the figurine, but Leena pulled him back down onto the sofa. She had both of her small arms locked around his. "What are you doing? Let me up." He tried to stand.

Leena leaned back into the sofa cushions, crossed one leg over his, and held him fast.

"What's she doing? Leena, let go of me."

The monk with the long ponytail of cherry-red hair stared at him with intense dark eyes.

Jakoby and Than chuckled.

"She likes you." Jakoby set the figurine down on the table. "You shouldn't fight it."

"Yes, don't fight it. That will only make her mad," Than added.

"What do you mean she likes me? Why would she like me?"

"It doesn't matter why. It only matters that she does," Than said. "Remember that."

"But she tried to kill me with those little sticks," Dyphestive said with a glance at Leena's belt. "I have little lumps on my skull. What are those sticks?"

"They are called nunchakus," Jakoby answered. "They're one of the many unique weapons that members of the Ministry of Hoods specialize in. Your friendly companion is a weapons master of sorts. It's primarily a discipline of her body, which I see you are getting very familiar with."

"I am not." Dyphestive tried to pull away even though he didn't mind Leena wrapping him up. "Leena, will you let go of me?"

He gave Than a pleading look. The hermit managed a grin and shrugged.

"Leena, I need to go after Grey Cloak. I'm not going to sit here and wait any longer."

"He'll be back," Than assured him. "But he carries too much on his shoulders. He needs to learn to rely on his companions more. Especially you, his blood brother. If he tries to do it all, it will only get worse. Trust me."

"It sounds like you're speaking from experience," Jakoby said. "And I agree. You have to be a team and trust each other."

"We've been together a long time, and one thing I know about Grey Cloak is he won't let me or Zora down. He'll die first. I would too." Leena hugged his arm tight. It looked like she might be smiling at him. "Jakoby, I have to report to Cleotus in the morning. Can you tell me about that?"

"Ah, Cleotus is lining you up to be a squire to the Monarch Knights or possibly a novice to the Honor Guard." Jakoby gave an approving nod as he stroked his moustache. "Cleotus is a good man—most all of them are —but make no mention of me. They will test you right away."

"How?"

"Even though I am a banished knight, I'm still bound by my oath, so you'll have to learn for yourself what that's all about. But something tells me you might surprise them more than they surprise you, seeing as you've been trained as a Doom Rider. Maybe try to keep your skill demonstrations to a minimum since you don't want to call too much attention to yourself."

Dyphestive hung his head. "Don't remind me. I want to forget all about being Iron Bones."

Than reached over and put a hand on his shoulder. "That's in the past, and it will always be a part of you. But use the skills they taught you to serve a greater good. Let that light shine inside you."

Than's words lifted the dark cloud hanging over Dyphestive's spirit. He felt so ashamed of his time with the Doom Riders and having killed the people he had as a result. It was a dark blot on his heart that he couldn't wipe off. "I'll try."

Jakoby pointed a finger at him. "The Honor Guard and Monarch Knights can teach you something about turning the darkness into light. They are stalwart men and women. I don't know how these events are going to unfold. It's risky trying to fool them, but make the most of your time with them, and try to be sincere." He clenched his fist. "Nothing is stronger than the bond between soldiers."

"Funny, the Doom Riders used to talk like that too," Dyphestive said.

"A man's actions determine his heart," Than offered. "Remember that."

Dyphestive nodded. "I'll try."

Leena elbowed him in the gut.

"Ow, what did you do that for, knobby elbow?"

Jakoby chuckled. "Apparently, your reply didn't convince her."

Dyphestive put his mouth right next to her ear and raised his voice. "I'll remember."

Leena nodded, and her eyes smiled. She suddenly stood up and pointed toward the door.

"What's happening?" he asked.

"I think Leena's getting antsy." Jakoby drained his coffee and set his mug on the table. He stood up and buckled on the sword belt hanging from the back of his chair. "I am too."

"So am I." Than placed Streak in Dyphestive's arms. He patted the dragon's head. "This little dragon likes the blood brothers. That's a good sign of things ahead. Take care of him, and he'll take care of you. Tell Grey Cloak we'll track him down later. Have faith."

All three of them headed for the door.

"Where are you going?"

"We'll try to figure out where Zora is." Jakoby winked. "In the meantime, get some rest. You'll need it for tomorrow."

The door closed.

Dyphestive sat with Streak tucked in his arms and the dragon's claws digging into his chest. He didn't even notice. He stretched out his hands and grabbed Codd. "I am Codd."

4

"Welcome!" the boar's head rug said the moment Grey Cloak stepped on it as he entered Batram's Bartery and Arcania.

Paying the hoarse-voiced rug no mind, he sauntered toward the bartery's display counters. Batram was nowhere to be seen, but a tall older man with long gray hair, wearing ruffled and well-worn gray robes, peered down at him with all-knowing eyes.

They stared at each other in the awkward silence without introducing themselves. The venerable man seemed to look right into Grey Cloak's soul as he leaned on a gnarled wooden staff that was almost as tall as he was.

Grey Cloak's eyes started to water, and he glanced away. He noticed a finely crafted short sword lying across the glass display counter. Rocking back and forth on his heels, he said, "That's a nice sword." He looked the older man up and down. "Are you trading up from that ugly staff?"

With his intense eyes glued to Grey Cloak's, the older man said, "No, I'm keeping the staff, for it keeps me upright when I'm upside down. And I don't have a need for the sword anymore. Not my style."

"I see. May I?" He reached for it.

As quick as a cat, the older man smacked him on the hand. "Hands off. I'm negotiating with this rogue."

Grey Cloak rubbed his stinging hand. "Good luck with that."

From way back in the shop, Batram the halfling waddled down the aisle between the tall ancient blackwood shelves and brass-handled drawers. The shop had a musty smell to it, and cobwebs covered the ceiling, nooks, and crannies. Spiders of all sorts and sizes crawled over them.

Without giving Grey Cloak a glance, Batram hopped up on the counter and stood eye to eye with the older wizardly fellow. He wore a black-and-white-striped vest, a red long-sleeved shirt, and had a yellow daisy in his front pocket. The cotton-headed halfling rubbed his fluffy goatee and eyed the short sword that shone in front of his bare feet. "I've thought about it and checked my inventory, and I've not seen the likes of that sword in this world. I'll give you five hundred gold chips for it."

"Five hundred! Outrageous! I didn't travel across the

universe to be insulted!" the older man said. "Five thousand chips. Not one chip less!"

Batram wrung his hands. "One thousand. That's the best I can do." He shrugged his narrow shoulders. "The truth is, there isn't a very big market for an enchanted short sword. It would be a tough sell."

The older man got nose to nose with Batram. "Your offer stings, Batram. I'll do it for fifteen hundred. Not one chip less."

"Sold!"

Before Grey Cloak could blink, Batram's quick little hands whisked the sword underneath the counter and replaced it with a full leather bag of chips the size of his head. "Oof! It's all there. I promise."

The wizardly fellow snatched the bag of coins in his big hand. "It better be, or I'll be back, Batram." He gave Grey Cloak a hawkish look. "What are you gawking at? Let's see how you look after you've saved the world as many times as I have." He tapped the butt end of his staff on the ground, and with a puff of smoke, he vanished.

Batram coughed and fanned the smoke from his face. "I hate it when he does that." He instantly turned into a giant with eight spider arms and a tarantula head, wearing a striped vest. He turned his attention to Grey Cloak and drummed his tentacle-like fingers on the counter. "Now, what do you want, thief?"

5

"I hope you've come to return the Cloak of Legends to me." Batram wrung his eight spidery hands together. He stretched the bottom two out. "I'll take it now."

Grey Cloak pulled the cloak tighter around his body. "No, we're even. Besides, no one else can use it, so why do you want it? Can you use it?"

Batram pulled his hands back, but his hungry eyes were locked on the cloak. "No, but it has sentimental value to me."

"I don't think that's true." He hopped up on the counter and sat down. "I think you're tormented by the fact that you gave it to me in error only to find out later that it had power." He reached into one of the many pockets inside the cloak and pulled out a potion vial. One by one, he placed three glass cylinders with corks and wax-coated tops on the counter. One potion restored wounds, another was for shrinking, and the third he didn't know what its purpose was, but it had been given to him by the Gunthys. There was a fourth potion for flying. Dyphestive had that. "I want to sell these."

"Interesting." Batram reached for the potions.

Grey Cloak pulled them away. "I want ten thousand gold chips."

Batram laughed. He tossed his head back and belly laughed harder and louder. The boar's head rug on the floor started up in rollicking laughter as well.

Grey Cloak's cheeks flushed. "Fine, if you aren't interested, I'll take them somewhere else." He started to slide them off the counter, but Batram seized him.

"Don't be so hasty, young one. I didn't say I wasn't interested. I only laughed at your ludicrous price. I'll give you five hundred. A very fair price."

"No, ten thousand."

Batram rolled his eyes. "I've been in the business for a very long time. I see all sorts and kinds. I can judge people. You're desperate, Grey Cloak. Tell me, what do you need ten thousand pieces of gold for?" He leaned on two sets of his elbows and shrugged his weird eyebrows over his bug eyes. "Tell me, what do you need a king's ransom for? A kidnapping?"

Grey Cloak turned hot under the collar. "What do you know?"

"Ah, so it is a ransom." Batram sucked his teeth and took a seat. "Take no offense. I don't have knowledge outside these doors other than that which is brought in to me. You aren't the first one to cross my threshold to save a friend. I've seen that desperate look in all sorts." He transformed back into a halfling and sat on the counter. "Tell me more."

"I don't see the point in it."

"Come now, I might have valuable insight. Humor me."

Batram was right about one thing. Grey Cloak was desperate, and he needed all the help he could get. He spent the next several minutes telling the halfling everything about Irsk Monco and his plan to steal Codd's shield. He was exhausted by the time he finished, and with his shoulders dipping, he said, "My head hurts from thinking about it."

"Interesting." Batram smoked a pipe that a pair of huge tarantulas had brought over to him while Grey Cloak was talking. He blew out a stream of smoke. "Very interesting."

"Is that all you have to say? Any advice?"

"I have plenty of advice, but that isn't free either."

He had a sudden urge to swat Batram upside the head. But deep down, he respected the way the little man did business. "How much?"

"How much advice do you want?"

"Enough to tell me what to do. Zooks, you're greedy. I thought we were friends."

"No, this is business. Friends help one another for free."

"I don't have time for this." He slid off the counter and headed for the door.

"You don't have much time at all." Batram's voice lowered to a hungry whisper. "Tell me, do you still have the Figurine of Heroes?"

Grey Cloak turned on his heel. "Yes. How much will you loan me for it?"

"I'll loan you one thousand chips. I'll buy it for five."

"I see." He approached the counter. *Let's see how much he'll pay for everything.* "So, five hundred for the potions. Five thousand for the figurine." He eyeballed Batram. "In gold?"

"Yes, in gold."

He dusted off his cloak in showy fashion. "How much for the cloak?"

"The cloak is mine. I'm letting you borrow it. You won't get a chip from me for it," Batram answered bitterly.

"No, it's my cloak. You gave it to me. I thought we were even on this." He ground his teeth. He was getting used to Batram and learning from him too. He was getting a better idea of what his enchanted items were worth. And the truth was, he enjoyed the haggling. "Well, I'm certain what you would pay wouldn't be enough. Plus, I'm not going to give up my dragon to Irsk. Chances are, he won't honor the deal either way."

"Perhaps he will. Perhaps he won't," Batram responded through his cloud of smoke. "One never knows the heart of another man's intentions. That was free advice, my friend. Remember it." He scratched the sideburn on his cheek and stretched out his stumpy arms. "If you steal the shield, and he doesn't take it, I'd be very interested in acquiring it. I'd like the entire suit actually. I know someone in the market for it. If you snatch any interesting pieces, bring them to me."

"You sound confident that I can do this."

Batram dangled his short legs over the counter and offered the palm of his hand. "Let me have the vial, the black one that you can't identify."

Grey Cloak reached into his pocket and withdrew the vial filled with churning black liquid. He hesitated and said, "For advice."

Batram nodded and took the potion vial. "Open your hand. These are flashings." He sprinkled several acorn-sized pellets into Grey Cloak's hand. With a sparkle in his eyes, he said, "Now you have everything you need."

An unseen force whisked Grey Cloak off his feet and flung him through the wide-open front door and onto the street.

"Hurry back!" the boar's head rug said.

He caught one last look at Batram waving before the

red door slammed shut, and the entire building vanished before his eyes.

"That dirty chipmunk got my potion for a handful of acorns!" He kicked the loose gravel on the street. "I have everything I need, my behind!" He stormed down the road.

6

THE SHELF

Anya's dragon blade sliced down in an arc of flashing light. The sharp metal sliced deep into the body of an enormous centipede with a lizard's head. The monster was as long as she was and as thick as her thigh, and its ugly plum-colored body had coiled around her leg. She sliced it again, splitting its shell in two. "Uck! Get off me!" She kicked the thick carcass away.

Three more lizarpedes scurried out of the dry hole in the dusty ground. They moved like snakes, with thousands of tiny legs rapidly propelling them forward from underneath. With flat heads like salamanders and sharp jackal teeth, they pursued her with their jaws opened wide.

Anya climbed higher onto the rocks of the barren landscape. "Come on, you dirty worms! Come!" She slashed the nearest lizarpede in twain and sent its gooey innards flying.

She butchered the next one's face as it crawled up the rock. "Taste my thunder!"

The third, and last, lizarpede coiled at the bottom of the rock. Small spines popped out of its wriggling back and shot toward her. Tiny black spikes filled the air.

She crouched down and covered her face behind the metal of her armor's bracers. The spikes bounced off with a sound like the loud pitter-patter of rain. She dropped her guard and caught another barrage of needles in her face. "Ugh!" she cried out. "That's it!"

Her jaw tightened as she stared down the monster. She leapt off the rock and landed right on top of it. Her steel-shod boots crushed through the monster's ringed exoskeleton and smooshed into the gummy parts of its body. She sliced its head off with a backhand swing.

Tiny spikes, like a porcupine's, stuck out of her face. They burned like fire. She leaned back against the boulder and started pulling the thin spikes out, one by one. The needles had little barbs that clung to her skin. She ground her teeth.

Cinder popped up from behind a rise. The grand dragon had a lizarpede hanging from his jaws. He sucked it in like a wet noodle, and his big eyes brightened when he saw more of the monsters lying dead on the deck. "Ah, more sustenance. I thank you, Anya. Well done. This is much easier than digging them out of their holes."

"I'm so glad I could be bait for you," she said in a dry voice.

Cinder scooped the parts of two more lizarpedes from the dusty deck and guzzled them down. "Mmmm... not the same as meat but very satisfying. Shall I save you some?"

She made an icky face. "No, I want you to have it. After all, you worked so hard for it."

"You sound bitter. Perhaps you are hungry." He nudged a lizarpede toward her feet with the horn of his nose. "Eat. It's good."

"I've eaten enough things that creep and crawl in this water-forsaken land." She wiped the goo off her sword with a rag. "But it felt good killing something. I needed it."

Cinder slurped down another lizarpede.

Anya's stomach turned. "That's disgusting. I need to remind myself not to look." She sheathed her blade and slid down to her seat. Her long beautiful hair was matted and hanging over her shoulder, and her sunburnt skin peeled and cracked. She couldn't remember the last time she'd properly bathed. Eyeing the sky, she said, "What does one have to do to get a breeze in this suffocating land?"

Cinder blew at her. His breath was warm, like a fresh-baked biscuit's, but it smelled like rotten lizarpede guts.

She pinched her nose. "No thank you, no thank you. You're making it worse."

"Sorry," he said politely as he laid his huge body down

on the ground at her feet like a loyal hound. "We could take a flight."

"Not now." She closed her eyes and rested her head against a rock. "Maybe tonight."

Anya and Cinder had been on the run and hiding for the better part of a year. Since the Sky Riders had been wiped out by Black Frost and his force, they'd been seeking refuge. They'd started with the Wizard Watch near Littleton, south of Gold Hook. They'd told the strange and aloof wizards what had happened. The brooding men and women in robes had received their message with looks as stony as the rocks that surrounded them and had coldly brushed them off.

The Wizard Watch infuriated Anya. She'd shaken her fist in their faces and left quickly, as she was completely uncertain of whose side they were on.

That left her and Cinder to care for the twelve fledgling dragons that had survived Black Frost's flame at Hidemark on Gunder Island. The fledglings were hidden in one of the plethora of caves that littered the Shelf. But the dragons grew fast, and hiding in the Shelf provided little to eat. It made their job all the more troublesome.

Anya plucked a spike out of her forehead that she'd missed. She eyed Cinder. The big dragon's stony lids were closed. If it hadn't been for his steadfast friendship, she didn't know what she would have done. He had been her rock. To make matters worse, he'd become the last one of his kind, a grand, unless one of the fledglings blossomed late. Otherwise, they were all middlings. But as the dragons grew bigger, it became harder to hide an entire thunder of them, which brought them to this desolate place.

"Cinder," she quietly said.

He opened one eye. "Yes, my dear?"

"Can you take care of the fledglings without me?"

He lifted his head. "You know I can. Anya, what are you planning to do?"

"You know I'd never leave you voluntarily, but traveling north is too risky for all of us. Black Frost will sniff us out for certain. Even if he thinks we're still alive, I don't think he's worried about us starving to death down here."

"What do you propose?"

She stood slowly. "I'm going north. I don't know why, but my gut is telling me I have to find Grey Cloak."

7

MONARCH CITY

Late that night, Grey Cloak entered Crane's apartment and found Dyphestive sleeping on the sofa, with his Codd figurine resting on his rising and falling chest. He snored softly. Streak was curled up underneath the big youth's feet, propping them up like a pillow.

Thank goodness everyone else is gone.

Several candles lining the walls of the room had melted down to nubs, but they provided a warm and welcoming illumination. He pulled off his leather boots. They were the same pair Zora had sold him the second time they officially met, when she helped dress him. He could still see her pretty face and big green eyes. It made him smile inside.

I'm going to save you, Zora. I promise.

The window overlooking the streets was open, and a gentle breeze stirred the cotton sheers. He sat down at the small kitchen table and started removing items from his enchanted pockets. The pockets were so deep that he could fit a sword inside one and not feel as if it were there at all.

The Cloak of Legends was interesting. If an item was too wide to fit in the pocket slit, the cloak would gobble it down—so to speak—like a great fish. All the while it kept him cozy, never too hot and never too cold, and as long as he wore it, his footfalls were as silent as if he were barefoot.

As he emptied his pockets, he reflected. He'd wandered the streets for hours trying to come up with a plan. According to Batram, he had everything he needed. He set the flashings on the table. They might have been the size of acorns, but they were as round as river stones and had tiny runes carved into them. He found it hard to believe that the stones were all he needed. He had five of them, but he'd tested them in an alley by tossing each on the ground. They made blinding flashes that dazzled him for moments.

I'm not so sure that's a big help. For a getaway perhaps.

He set a potion for wound restoration and a potion for shrinking on the table. He rolled the restoration potion between his fingers and watched the sparkling yellow fluid twist like a tiny tornado. He flipped it from one hand to the other.

I don't see how this will help.

During his long stroll, he caught on to what Batram meant when he said that Grey Cloak already had every-thing he needed. He realized that Batram wasn't talking about the flashings but everything else. The potions, his cloak, the figurine, his friends, that was all he needed, that and a good plan. He'd been bending his mind, trying to come up with something that might work before they reported to Captain Cleotus on the morrow.

He set the Figurine of Heroes between the two potion vials that he'd stood on their corks. He studied the faceless humanoid made out of black onyx. He recalled the words that ignited the enchantment in his mind—he always did once a day—and made sure that he never uttered it out loud. The powerful magic was both dangerous and exhilarating at the same time.

Perhaps this is all I need.

Of course, the Figurine of Heroes summoned powerful heroes from another world who quickly dished out punishment. He didn't think that would work in Monarch Castle. Jakoby said the guards were good people and that he shouldn't cross them. Grey Cloak had to come up with another plan, a plan that was subtle and nonviolent.

I think I can fool the guards, but how can I fool the yonders?

Dyphestive stirred. His Codd figurine rolled off his chest and plunked onto the floor. He sat up, bright-eyed and bushy-tailed, and eyed Grey Cloak. "You're back."

"I haven't been here long. Are you resting up for your day tomorrow?"

Dyphestive scooped his figurine off the floor. "I'm ashamed to admit it, but I'm excited."

"We're doing this for Zora, not ourselves."

"I know that. But I'm curious." Dyphestive eyeballed his figurine. "Ah, the shield fell off!" He bent over and jammed his fingers under the sofa. "There it is, I think."

"You better get it before Streak does. He'll squirrel it away with his hoard."

"I have it." Dyphestive held the tiny shield up proudly between his thumb and index finger. "Just like the real thing but smaller."

Grey Cloak's gray eyes widened like saucers. With a devilish smirk, he sat up. "That's it!"

8

MONARCH CASTLE

"Bloody Monarch Knights think they own this castle," Airius said as he led Grey Cloak through the castle's corridors. In a snobbish voice, the elven head servant continued. "I'm in charge of the servants, not them. They always see fit to make my choices for me." The short and rawboned elf turned his chin over his shoulder and looked back at Grey Cloak. "At least you're an elf."

Grey Cloak trailed behind the refined man's slow and unique gait. Airius's arms shoveled out in front of him as he walked, his torso leaning back in an odd balancing act. Airius was older, and he didn't move very fast, but his black clothing was neatly pressed, and his silver buttons and cuff links shone like the morning sun.

Beside Grey Cloak was another servant, Sayma. She was an attractive elf, young like him, with silvery-white hair tied back in a straight ponytail, with black ribbons woven into it. She wore black garb with a white apron and had a white servant's cap on her head. She maintained a serious expression.

Airius opened a door in the alcove underneath a stairwell near the bustling kitchens. It was morning, and Captain Cleotus had introduced Grey Cloak to Airius only minutes ago. It had been a quick introduction, and Captain Cleotus had whisked Dyphestive away to the Honor Guard's training grounds.

A set of stairs led down into a dormitory of small rooms. Each room held two small beds with wooden chests at their feet. Airius reached down and opened a chest. "You can store your belongings in this chest, and this will be your bed. It will always be made when you're not sleeping in it. I want the corners tight." A silver chip appeared in his hand. He bounced it off the bed's woolen blanket and snatched it away. Airius had a way of looking down at Grey Cloak even though he had to look up. "Very tight. You can make a bed, can't you?"

"Yes," Grey Cloak replied.

"And don't smirk. I don't like smirking. I don't like smiling either. We're here to serve, not be happy." Airius combed Grey Cloak's hair behind his ears. "Hmm... you're a bit shaggy but well-knit. Good cheekbones. Tell me, have you served before, as Captain Cleotus, the oaf, said?"

Grey Cloak nodded.

"We'll see. Sayma, find him a uniform, but take him to the barber first. I want him serving this morning. I want to know if he has the chops to do this or not." He slowly turned around and walked out of the room in his strange gait.

Grey Cloak did a quick imitation of Airius. He mimicked his walk. "I don't like smirking. And I don't like smiling either."

Sayma didn't crack a smile.

"Sorry," he said guiltily, recognizing Airius's no-nonsense expression in her features. "I didn't realize you two were related."

The soft-angled features of her straight face broke into a smile, and she burst into warm laughter. Holding her belly, she dropped down on the bed. "Oh my goodness, that's the best imitation of Airius I've ever seen. You did him perfectly." She popped up and peeked around the door. "Good, he's gone. You have to be careful with the old man. He likes to linger." She extended her hand. "Let me formally introduce myself. My name is Sayma."

He squeezed her warm hand with both of his. "I'm Grey Cloak."

"You were named after a garment?"

"Why does everyone say that?"

"Isn't it obvious?" She pulled on the shoulder of his cloak. "You weren't born in that thing, were you?"

"No."

"Here, let me help you out of that. As much as I'd like to chat, we need to get moving, or Airius will be on us like flies on dung."

"Good to know."

She tousled his hair with her slender fingers. She wore a faint but pleasant flowery fragrance. As she ran her hands over his shoulders and body, she said, "Don't get any ideas. I'm sizing you up for your uniform. But Airius is right. You are well-built."

"I know."

Sayma smiled. "Come on, let's trim those bangs and get you suited up. We can't keep the dubious Monarchs waiting." She led him from the room and down the long, narrow hall adorned with wooden doors to the servants' quarters. They squeezed by other servants coming and going and finally made it to a back room with a gnome standing on a high stool, who quickly trimmed his hair.

After the haircut, they made their way to the uniform closet, which had wooden shelves loaded with shirts, pants, dresses, aprons, and boots. Sayma pressed a set of clothing into his arms. "This will do." She led him back to his room. "Hurry up. Chop-chop. The Monarchs are waiting."

"A little privacy, please?"

She rolled her eyes. "And I thought you weren't shy."

"Not shy, only modest." He closed the door to change, and in seconds, he looked like he belonged, the same as the other servants. He folded up the Cloak of Legends and the clothing Zora had picked out for him. He focused on the mission. He had a plan. Now all he had to do was execute it.

Must save Zora. Only two days to go.

He couldn't find a way to lock his footlocker. *Zooks.* "Uh, Sayma, don't these boxes have locks?"

"No, none of us have anything to steal, and by the looks of it, you don't either."

I don't know about that.

He flattened his cloak and hid it underneath his mattress.

Sayma knocked on the door. "Are you taking a nap?"

He flung the door open with a smile. "I'm ready."

She chuckled. "We'll see about that."

9

Dyphestive stood at attention in the small courtyard of the Honor Guard's training grounds. Two elven men stood to his right, and a human man and woman stood to his left. He stood half a head taller than the tallest of the strapping people, all of whom were well put together. They'd been given padded-leather chest plates, and each held a jo stick. All eyes were on the soldier standing before them, a member of the Honor Guard, complete with scale mail armor and a golden sash. The man was broad faced, flat nosed, and clean-shaven, with thinning, wavy brown hair hanging past his ears and a stout but squatty build. The whites of his eyes shone like he was crazy.

"My name is Tinison! Sergeant Tinison!" He spit when he spoke. His harsh voice was loud. "I don't know what wormhole the likes of you were dragged out of, but I aim to stuff you back in!" He marched up to Dyphestive and stood nose to nose with him. "Do you find me amusing, boy!"

"No, Sergeant!"

"Then why are you smiling?"

"I'm not. I always look like this... I think."

"Listen here, Baby Face. I've seen big boys like you waltz in here like they're going to be king of the world only to run out of here crying like halflings." Sergeant Tinison bumped chests with Dyphestive. "I don't know what Captain Cleotus was thinking, dragging you to me. I'm going to turn your big bones into goo! Do you agree?"

"Er—"

"My name's not ER! It's SERGEANT TINISON! Answer me! Answer me!"

Dyphestive swallowed the lump building in his throat and shouted back in the sergeant's face. "No!"

Sergeant Tinison rose on tiptoe. "Are you yelling at me?"

"Yes!"

"Did I give you permission to yell at me?"

"No!"

"Stop yelling at me!" Sergeant Tinison fingered his ear, cocked his head to one side, and casually moved to the elf standing beside Dyphestive. "The big boy has some lungs on him, doesn't he?"

"Yes, Sergeant," the elf said in an agreeable tone.

Dyphestive could see the elf was gaining the sergeant's confidence out of the corner of his eye.

Sergeant Tinison nodded, his big chin bobbing. He put a hand on the elf's shoulder and gave him the once over. "Say, you're an elf, aren't you?"

The elf puffed out his chest and said in a more confident tone, "Yes, Sergeant."

Sergeant Tinison got in his face. "I hate elves! I hate your ears and your pretty little features. I hate your tiny little noses. Look at my nose, elf! Look at it! Do you like it? Tell me, do you like it?"

"Yes!" the elf said in a shaky voice.

"You're lying to me! I hate my nose! It's been broken eight times! Look at it! Look at it!" The sergeant moved over to the only female in the group. "What do we have here?" He touched her chestnut-brown hair. "A female." He crossed his arms. "How nice. Tell me, what are you?"

"Pardon, Sergeant?" she asked.

"I said, what... are... you?"

"I don't understand the question."

Sergeant Tinison's voice rose to new heights. "I'll tell you what you are. You're an overachiever. That's what you are! A woman in the Honor Guard? Is that a jest?" He got in her face. "Is it? Is it? Is it? Answer me! Say it! Say it! Say it! Auuuuuuuuugh! Say it!"

"It's not a jest, Sergeant. I've seen other women in the Honor Guard," she said.

Sergeant Tinison punched her in the belly and dropped her to her knees. He screamed in her ear, "They aren't women! They're Honor Guard!"

BY MIDAFTERNOON, the hot sun was beating down on the Honor Guard trainees like a dragon's breath. They'd soaked through their padded-leather armor, and they marched behind Sergeant Tinison with their heads low except for Dyphestive.

The strapping youth kept his chin up and a humble smile on his face. He'd been through worse, much worse with the Doom Riders, who made him push wheelbarrows full of rocks up a mountainside. The calisthenics and the hard running were routine to him. The weapons training was rudimentary as well. Sergeant Tinison hadn't shown him anything he hadn't seen before, and it was driving the sergeant crazy.

Dyphestive had finished his one hundredth push-up with Sergeant Tinison on the ground yelling in his ear. "Is that all you can do, Baby Face? Don't you have more in you?"

Dyphestive did ten more and kept going. Sweat dripped off his chin, but he could do one hundred more if he had to. He suddenly remembered what Jakoby had told him about blending in and not overly demonstrating his well-honed skills. He decided to take a break and collapsed on the ground.

"Look at this! A quitter! Same as that elf who tucked tail and scurried out of here!" Sergeant Tinison said. "Quit now. Run home, and you'll be back in time for Mother's dinner. I bet she'll have a big hug and kiss waiting for you."

"I don't have a mother," Dyphestive muttered.

"Oh, boo-hoo, orphan boy!" Sergeant Tinison smacked him on the back of the head. "How about this, loser? I'll be your mother! Loser! Loser! Loser! Auuuugh! Auuuugh! Loser! Get up, Baby Face. Get up! The orphan snatchers are coming!"

Dyphestive bounced to his feet and glared down at Sergeant Tinison. "You're not very nice."

Sergeant Tinison clapped his thick hands together. "That's the smartest thing you've said all day, Baby Face." He glanced sideways at the young woman in the group. She had a crooked nose. "Beak! Fetch the sticks. It's time to see which one of you has enough stones to be an Honor Guard."

10

Jakoby, Leena, and Than sat in the pews of Monarch City's main cathedral. The Cathedral of Saints was a massive structure, capable of hosting thousands, with tremendous stone archways holding up the hundred-foot-high ceilings. An occasional dove flew overhead and roosted in the nests of the archways. Stained glass windows decorated the walls, and bright sunlight shone fully through the purple and ruby-red glass with eerie effect. Monks in drab, loose-fitting clothing sauntered between the long swath of pews, offering to help the needy people who entered and sat down.

"I'm not so certain this is the best idea," Jakoby said to Than as he drew his hood higher over his face. His skin prickled at the thought of the dungeons below, where he'd been locked up. "Do you really think it's wise to go back?"

Than cleared his throat. "This is where Orpah came and went. It's the only advantage we have."

A big-eared monk teetered over and offered them a donation basket.

Than waved him off. "If we had money, we wouldn't be here. We're hungry."

Jakoby watched the monk move out of earshot. The large cathedral had many people scattered all over the parish, perhaps a hundred or more, but the place was so large, it appeared barren. "Do you really think they would keep Zora in the same place they kept us? That seems obvious."

Leena, who sat on the other side of Jakoby, leaned forward and glared at Than.

"True, it might be a trap, or it might be the last place they think we would look." Than winked at Leena.

She stuck her tongue out at him.

"I don't suppose we're going to sit here all day," Jakoby said as he rose. "Let's pay our jailers a visit."

He led the way to the front of the cathedral and moved up onto the stage. Several candles burned on a tiered stand in front of an enormous statue of a man in flowing robes with a solid-gold sun for a face. He lit a dry candle wick with another candle while a nearby monk stood by, staring. He nodded at the long-faced man, who headed his way.

"Are you lost, young man?" the monk asked in a haunting voice.

"In a manner of speaking, you might say that." Jakoby put his arm over the fragile man's shoulders. He walked the man beyond the curtains toward the back. "You see, I've been wandering the streets a long time, trying to find a purpose. Could you give me guidance?"

"Of course. We're always looking for volunteers to serve the needy. Willing servants of the sun gods."

"This is a big place. If I volunteer, do you have somewhere for me and my friends to stay?"

The monk squeezed Jakoby's strong shoulders. "You are well-made. If you use that brawn, we will board you, but only long enough for you to get back on your feet. Come with me."

Jakoby nodded at Than and Leena. They quietly followed.

The monk led them to a storage room located down the stairs in the back of the cathedral. They passed a labyrinth of small rooms.

"There." The monk pointed from just inside the doorway. "Find a set of robes. Dress. I'll return, and we'll swear you in."

The moment they turned to look at the robes hanging on the walls, the monk slammed the door closed.

Jakoby rushed to the heavy wooden door and tugged on the handle. "That spooky snake handler locked us in!"

Than donned a set of monk's robes, and Leena did the same.

Jakoby stroked his moustache. "Do you really think we're going to fool them by playing dumb?"

"It got us this far, didn't it?" Than asked.

"Are you suggesting we get ourselves thrown in the dungeon? I'm not getting locked back up. No thank you," Jakoby said. "Leena, pick this lock, and get us out of here."

Leena hurried over to the door and pulled a hairpin from the neck of her ponytail. As Jakoby dressed, she picked the lock.

"I'm not putting the cuffs back on. I'll fight and die first."

"Great words to live by," Than said. "You're doing exactly what I thought you would."

Leena opened the door, and the trio entered the hall.

"It won't be long before they figure out we escaped, and this place is crawling with monks and whatever else."

Than closed the door, stuck a long yellow finger in the keyhole, and zapped it with a charge of light. A tiny plume of smoke drifted out of the hole. "That conundrum should keep them busy." He stepped aside. "After you."

"Are you a wizard?" Jakoby asked as he led them down into the bowels of the cathedral.

"No."

"A druid?"

"No."

"Then what are you?"

"On your side. That's all that matters."

After several twists, turns, and backtracks through the network of corridors and staircases, they came to the dank levels deep below the surface. They stepped into a corridor of stone, slick from the water dripping from the ceiling. At the end of the corridor, a pair of burly lizardmen stood guard in front of an entry made of iron bars.

Jakoby's fingertips tingled as they went deeper. Disguised as monks, they moved over the watery floor, and he quietly said, "I'll handle this."

The lizardmen stood upright and jabbed their spears at them. "Halt!"

Jakoby lifted his hands and smiled. "Brethren, I exalt you." He dropped his hood and smiled. "I have a prisoner with me." He grabbed Than's arm and pulled him forward. "This old crone was caught stealing from the coffers. I was told to bring him to you. Will you take him?"

"A petty thief," the tallest lizardman said. "Hah. He's not worthy of our dungeons. If he stole from the sun gods, then there is only one thing to do. Execute him." Without warning, the lizardman thrust his spear and stabbed Than in the chest.

Jakoby couldn't hide his shock as Than dropped to a knee. Jakoby fumbled for the sword underneath his robes and pulled it free just as the second lizardman attacked, shouting, "Intruder!"

11

"Try to keep up," Sayma said to Grey Cloak. "We can't keep the Monarchs waiting. And remember, don't look at them directly, ever. Think of yourself as a piece of furniture. We serve. We vanish."

Grey Cloak hurried behind her, a silver serving tray loaded with covered platters of food on his shoulder. They traversed the hidden corridors that led from the kitchen to the castle's main interior rooms. It was a veritable labyrinth when he didn't know where he was going. He quickly picked up on it, however. "Are you telling me that you've never looked a single Monarch in the eye? I find that hard to believe."

"No, I haven't."

"I bet you have."

"Are you calling me a liar?"

"Come now, how could you not look? The finest people in Monarch City are gathered there."

She stopped, turned, and faced him. "Listen to me. You aren't going to last very long as a servant if you can't control your curiosity. I've caught you staring at the castle's guests. You need to watch it because *they* are watching." She glanced up.

"Oh, you mean the enchanters and the yonders, don't you?" he asked, fishing for information. "Captain Cleotus told us about them. Creepy. Do they bother you?"

"Doesn't being watched all the time bother you? I can't go into a room without seeing one. The only time I have any privacy is when I'm in my quarters." She tipped her head. "Come on."

They'd been on the go for hours, hustling back and forth between the kitchens and the dining and living rooms. Monarch Castle wasn't so much of a residence as it was a government where the leaders of the city and the Monarchs' guests gathered. The entire day was a well-planned and tireless event.

"So, you can see the yonders even when they're hidden?"

"In time, you get an eye for it. You can feel them. Creepy things. The only way to avoid them is outside in the daylight."

"They don't like the sun?"

"It's an aversion to bright light. We'd probably have the same problem, too, if we were a giant eyeball."

Grey Cloak grinned. *Perfect.*

He followed Sayma's lead into one of the extravagant dining chambers. Ten men and women were sitting at an ivory dinner table painted with golden trim. As the group of dignitaries talked amongst themselves, they set the covered plates before them.

Grey Cloak couldn't believe his eyes. *Look at the wealth.* In such close proximity, he gained a quick feel for the people at the table. They wore lavish and gaudy jewelry. Their clothing was cut from the finest cloth and silk, and their perfume reeked of shameless spending.

He got a feel for the Monarchs as well. They always sat at the head of the table, at one end or the other or both. When they spoke, their guests quieted. They had a domineering presence but were polite and well spoken, and the guests at the table were quick to suck up to them.

After he and Sayma served the food, they both stepped back and stood on the side of the bay window. They stood as still as cranes, only moving to refill the silver goblets with wine. After half an hour, the Monarch at the end of the table, a woman in a full satin dress with a pillowy bottom, rang a crystal bell. Sayma and Grey Cloak quickly dismissed themselves behind the curtains and hustled down the hidden corridor.

"I'm glad that's over with. Come on," Sayma said.

"Where to now?"

"It's time to give my aching feet a break. We'll swing by the kitchen and grab some scraps to eat. Monley always sets something aside for me. I'll share." She eyed him. "Hungry?"

He patted his belly. "Famished." He couldn't remember the last time he'd eaten because, when he had, it hadn't been much, and he hadn't cared for it. But his hunger had caught up to him. Anything would be nice.

Sayma whizzed through the kitchens and grabbed a napkin stuffed with food from the end of a butcher-block prep table. "Thank you, Monley!" she shouted to a sandy-haired dwarven man hammering bread dough with his fists.

He winked at Sayma and glared at Grey Cloak.

Sayma grabbed a burning candle from a tabletop on her way. She led them up a narrow staircase into a small tower that overlooked one of the many castle gardens. It was a crammed lookout post with two three-legged stools and some dried scraps of bread on the floor. Sayma scooped up the bread scraps and set them on the ledge of the portal window. A yellow bird with white wings landed on the windowsill and pecked at the bread. Sayma opened her hand and fed the crow-sized bird. "This is Lenny. A garden bird. My best friend." She touched the bird's beak with her nose.

"That's interesting."

"Go ahead and eat. You sound like you're getting cranky." She fished a small pipe out of her pocket and stuffed a pinch of tobacco into it. Using the candle, she lit the pipe and huffed out smoke. She offered it to Grey Cloak. "I love the sweet aroma of tobacco. Care to try?"

"No thanks." He opened the cloth napkin and grabbed a biscuit, a strip of bacon, and a hunk of cheese. He loaded the bacon and cheese inside the biscuit. "Are you allowed to smoke a pipe?"

She shrugged and blew smoke out the window. "It keeps the yonders away. But Airius would kill me. Of course, most of us pipe smoke, and he can't do away with all of us." She gave him the mature look of a much older woman. "So, how do you like your first day?"

"I've had worse days," he admitted around a mouthful of food.

"Huh, many can't do this job. They quit a day or two into it, but you're doing very well. I'm impressed."

"Thanks."

"Now tell me, why are you really here?"

He lifted his gaze and met hers. "What do you mean?"

"I've been doing this awhile, and I'm a good judge of people. You're here for something else. What is it? And be honest, or I'll turn Airius onto you." She gave him a deadpan stare. "I'm serious."

He swallowed. "Well, if you must know, I'm here to steal Codd's shield."

"Get after it, you two bags of donkey dung!" Sergeant Tinison hollered. He crouched down with his hands on his knees, a menacing look on his face. "We're waiting. Somebody hit somebody! Do you want to be an Honor Guard or not?"

The four trainees stood amidst fifteen members of the Honor Guard, there to watch the new recruits, in what they called the Ring of Battle. Dyphestive stood among the stalwart men and women as well as a man he trained alongside named Hodges.

Inside the Ring of Battle, the woman Sergeant Tinison fondly called Beak squared off with the remaining elf trainee, named Fancy Feet. They both twirled their jo sticks and jabbed at each other.

"What's going on, Sergeant? Is this a dance or a fight?" a

gusty orcen female member of the Honor Guard asked. "Pitiful!"

"Stuff a fist in it, Tulip, before I do," Sergeant Tinison said. "If you don't want to watch, go braid your beard or something."

The Honor Guard erupted in throaty laughter.

Tulip grabbed her chin and blanched.

"Let's go, Fancy Feet! Quit twirling that stick around! What are you trying to do, fly away?" Sergeant Tinison clapped his hands. "Somebody make somebody bleed!"

Beak was quick, but Fancy Feet was quicker. She jabbed, he juked. Off and on, their jo sticks would clack together, and they would break away again.

Dyphestive had seen his fair share of fights in his lifetime, and this show was boring. The two fighters used the long lengths of wood like swords, but a well-trained weapons master could use them for more than that.

I shouldn't have any trouble whipping either of them.

"Whoo boy! Somebody get me some coffee because it's going to be a long time before one of these toads hurts the other. Why don't you both lie down, and we'll wait and see who dies first?" Sergeant Tinison thumbed the sweat from his eyes. "Come on, sandbags! My eyes are falling asleep!"

Beak went on the aggressive. She swiped at Fancy Feet's legs. He jumped over the long stick with ease. She jabbed, stepped, and lunged. He evaded with feathery ease and countered with a sideswipe of his own. Beak ducked underneath it.

"Oh my! Listen, everyone!" Sergeant Tinison cupped his ear. "It's the sound of boredom! Aaauuuuuuugh! Somebody hit someone!"

"You want a show? You shall have it!" Beak went berserk. She attacked Fancy Feet with a brutal but precise fury. Her sudden lunge with her jo stick slipped past the elf's quick reflexes and knocked him hard on the shoulder. He let out a pained groan.

Beak's onslaught ramped up. She busted his shin, jabbed his belly, and cracked her jo stick against the side of his head.

Fancy Feet staggered away on noodling legs.

The Honor Guard exploded into thunderous cheers.

Beak whipped Fancy Feet like a borrowed mule.

Crack! Smack! Chuk! Thok!

Fancy Feet didn't know what hit him. He frantically flailed away, but a fast swipe by Beak swept his feet out from under him, knocking him flat on his back.

Beak pounced on Fancy Feet. She pinned him underneath her thighs and put her jo stick against his throat. Red-faced, he pushed back against her jo stick for a moment then quickly tapped out. She screamed gutturally in his face before releasing him and stood to the sound of thunderous applause from her superiors. Even Sergeant Tinison had an approving sneer on his face.

Dyphestive couldn't clap loud enough. He had clearly underestimated Beak. She was good.

Sergeant Tinison gave Fancy Feet a kick on the rear as a pair of Honor Guards carried the broken and bloodied man out. "Let him dance with the moat monsters. Get the elf out of here!" He eyeballed Dyphestive and Hodges. "Get in the circle, you two hootenannies! And I better get a stronger start than the last one."

Dyphestive and Hodges squared off with their jo sticks in hand. Hodges had a heavy build and tired eyes, which gave him a lazy look. He was older than Dyphestive, built like a dwarf, and had short, coarse black hair and a beard that looked like a fuzzy helmet keeping his face safe.

Dyphestive nodded at him. "Good luck."

Hodges sneered back.

Sergeant Tinison shouted, "What are you waiting for? A bell to ring? Get after it!"

Dyphestive glanced at Sergeant Tinison. Hodges smacked him right upside the temple with his jo stick with a resounding *whack*. The precise blow made his legs wobble and dropped him to one knee. All he could hear was a sea of the Honor Guards' cheers lifting into the sky. He was hit again. *Whack! Whack! Whack!*

13

Leena flicked her nunchakus in the wink of an eye and smote both lizardmen across the jaw.

Chuk! Crack!

The iron-jawed lizardmen wobbled a moment before they straightened their backs. Leena rammed her knee into the shorter lizardman's groin, doubling him over, and cracked him in the earholes with her sticks. The lizardman dropped.

Jakoby sliced the tip off the taller lizardman's spear, which was still in Than's belly. As the lizardman went for his sword, Jakoby thrust his sword deep into the lizard-man's chest. "Mercy on him."

With both lizardmen down, they went to Than's aid. Than was on the ground, clutching his gut. "I'm fine. I'm fine."

"You aren't fine. You were stabbed in the gut," Jakoby said as he searched for the wound.

Than slapped his hands away and said in a cranky voice, "I'm fine. The lizardman caught me off guard is all, leaving me wounded with shame. I should have seen that coming." He stood up. "Let's get going."

"Hold on a moment." Jakoby picked up the end of the spear he'd severed. The point was bent. "Care to explain this?"

"It explains itself. The lizardman forgot to sharpen his spear. How lucky for me," Than said.

Leena snuck up to Than and lifted his clothing. She gasped quietly.

Jakoby dropped his gaze to Than's belly. It was covered in thick gray-and-black scales, like the man's arms and hands. It looked like snakeskin. "You're like that all over. What is that?"

"My business." Than grabbed the key ring from one of the guards and unlocked the gate. "We have a mission. Stop with the questions."

"Are you a lizardman?" he asked.

Than stopped and gave Jakoby a serious look. "Call me a lizardman, or even suggest it, and I'll wrap that sword around your neck."

Jakoby smiled tentatively. "Don't take it personally, old man. You're the one with scales. What was I supposed to think?"

"Think smart. Lizards aren't the only creatures with scales." Than jogged down the long corridor on feet as light as a feather. The passageway opened into an inner sanctuary of a larger network of rooms. "We're close. I can hear people screaming."

Jakoby didn't hear a thing, and Leena shrugged her eyebrows at him. "Why don't you lead the way?"

"A good idea." Than took off like a ghost.

Jakoby had a hard time keeping up with the scruffy-looking man who moved like a will-o'-the-wisp. Than would rush to a spot and duck into an alcove or room while lizardman soldiers marched right by him. Than clearly had more to him than met the eye.

With the coast clear, Jakoby said, "What are we supposed to do, waltz down to the dungeons and do roll call?"

Than clawed at the ends of his hair. "I hadn't really thought this far into it. But your idea is sound. I like it."

"What idea, roll call?"

Than pointed inside a storage room. "Grab some buckets, shovels, and pans. We have some cleaning to do. Come on."

The trio ventured down a wide stone staircase that led to the very heart of the same dungeon that they had escaped from. At the very bottom of the stairs, the iron gate was closed. A lizardman guard sat snoring in a chair leaned back on two legs against the wall. He was stationed by the lever that opened the gate.

Beyond the gate, four lizardmen made their rounds. Six cages hung suspended over the floor, and at the far end on the left, a four-armed ogre sat on the ground, with his head between his knees.

Jakoby pressed his face to the bars. "I don't see her. Do you?"

Than's nostrils flared. "I don't see or smell her, but I can't be certain. My senses are not what they once were here. We need to get inside." He rapped his knuckles gently on the gate.

The lizardman leaning in the chair opened his eyelids. His yellow eyes slid over to the trio on the other side of the gate. He wiped drool from his mouth and dropped the two raised chair legs to the floor. Rubbing his eyes, he approached. "What do you want?" the husky-voiced lizardman asked.

Than nudged Jakoby. Jakoby cleared his throat and improvised. "We come to do our service to the sun gods. We come to clean. To serve. To ease the burden on your shoulders," he said in a soft, awkward voice. He raised a bucket and brush. "We clean."

"I've heard nothing about this." The lizardman eyed the trio warily. "Who sent you?"

"The sun gods," Jakoby innocently said.

"Bloody moons, I don't have time for this." He shouted

down the stairs, "Haavers! Do you know about a monk cleanup? Apparently, the sun gods sent them!"

The brood of lizardmen broke out in hissing laughter.

"Of course, send them in."

"Ah, stifle yourself! You just don't want to clean!"

"None of us want to clean! We say let them in, Adsel!" Haavers shouted back.

"Bloody moons!" Adsel grabbed the lever and pushed it up. He hollered back over his shoulder, "You better keep a close eye on them! This watch can't foul up like the last one."

The iron gate rattled upward.

The trio stepped past the threshold.

Adsel pulled the lever and closed them inside. "Get at it, and don't be down there trying to convert those people. You clean. I want none of the warm and friendly treatment, or I'll send you out of here with your heads tucked between your legs."

"Where should we start?" Jakoby asked.

Adsel the lizardman sat down, leaned his chair back against the wall, and smiled. "You want to clean? Then start in the ogre's grove." He closed his eyes and laughed. "Hah-hah."

As they walked down the stairs, Than said under his breath, "Try to split up and search the cages. By the way, that was some pretty good acting. Have you done it before?"

"Acted? No. Been a sun-god monk? Yes," Jakoby said,

shamefaced. "Don't ask. You two take the front. I'll move back to the ogre's den." He eyeballed the suspended cages along the way. No one in the cages resembled Zora. He made a beeline for the ogre's lair, walking by the dungeon cells on the way down, and peered inside each one.

The prisoners were in awful shape. Their stomachs groaned as their sunken eyes locked on Jakoby. A feeling of dread came over him. It was the same feeling he'd had when he was a prisoner before Grey Cloak, Dyphestive, and Zora came. He owed them. He owed her. He didn't see any sign of her on his way to the ogre's lair.

The four-armed ogre didn't budge from his spot. Jakoby pinched his nose as he stood at the threshold of the big humanoid's den. *This is awful. Nothing could clean this.* He ventured a foot inside. The den was a deep cave, big enough for three ogres to huddle in. He dug his shovel into the grit and started scooping the waste. He loaded up a bucket and headed to the fire pit, with his nose tucked into his robes. *Ugh, this is awful.*

A deep stone fire pit where all of the waste could be burned sat at the back of the dungeon row. He met up with Than and Leena by the stones. "Did you find her?"

"No," Than said as he dumped his bucket into the fire. "I take it you came up empty-handed as well."

"I didn't see her. I say we move on before these green toads sniff us out," Jakoby responded.

"Agreed." Than headed toward the steps leading out. As

soon as his foot stopped on the bottom step, the stone landing erupted in smoke.

The trio moved back and watched with big eyes as the smoke faded. Six warriors wearing iron masks and crimson robes stood tall on the platform. They were accompanied by a bald man with sunken eyes and vulturelike features. He wore black robes with a tight collar, and he stared the trio down with haunting eyes. "I am Finton Slay. These are the Iron Devils. I've been expecting you." He stepped away from the masked men. "Kill them."

14

Sayma belly laughed so hard she fell off her stool. "You really are a jester." The flummoxed young woman tilted her stool back onto its legs. "You really shouldn't joke about something like that though. If the wrong person hears it, you'll be fed to the moat monsters."

"Do they really feed people to the moat monsters? And I'm not joking."

"Hah. You don't know when to quit, do you, little Grey Cloak?" She pinched his cheek. "But I admire your ambition. Tell me, if you stole the shield, what would you do with it? Sell it for a fortune?"

"No, I thought it would look really good in my quarters." He smirked.

She giggled. "I don't think there's room for it." She tapped her pipe ashes out over the windowsill. The garden bird flew away. She crumbled up a biscuit and left it on the windowsill. "Come on."

"But you didn't eat anything."

"I save my tummy for dinner. I just wanted to feed you and the birds." She put her pipe away and dusted off her apron. "Did you get enough to eat?"

"Plenty."

"Good, you're going to need plenty of energy if you're going to steal Codd's shield. Tell me, how would you do it?"

"Ah, I can't tell you that," he said on his way down the stairs.

"Why, because you'll have to kill me?"

"No, because I don't know yet."

She nudged him with her shoulder. "You're funny. I hope you stick around."

He nodded and took a step back. "So long as they will have me." He almost bumped into Airius at the bottom of the stairs. He quickly hopped away. "Excuse me, sorry."

"I've been looking for you two," Arius said with disappointment. "Come with me, both of you." He led them through the busy kitchen to a small neatly organized office in the back. "Close the door and sit."

Sayma had a nervous look in her eye as she closed the door and sat down in a small wooden chair beside Grey Cloak.

Airius glanced down his nose at them but focused his

attention on Sayma. "How is this newcomer handling his duties?"

She sat up and leaned forward. "Very well. He's proven to be an apt and quick learner."

"Very good." Airius scribbled notes on a parchment with a feather quill he dipped in an inkwell. "Is he capable of backing up your duties?"

"I'm confident he could master all of them over time." She rubbed her hands on her apron and chewed her lip. "He's very apt."

"Yes, you said that." Airius opened a wooden drawer and produced a small coin purse. He tossed it to the end of his desk in front of Sayma. "Take that."

She grabbed the coin purse and glanced at Grey Cloak. She seemed to shrink in her seat, and with a shaky voice she asked, "Headmaster, what is this for?"

"It's called severance pay. The monarchy is releasing you from your services."

She gasped and sobbed. "But why?"

"Why? You need to ask why, you little pipe smoker? I warned you about that." Airius shoved a parchment and quill over to Grey Cloak. "I need you to sign this. You're a witness."

"Uh, um, but—"

"Sign it, or I'll show you the door too."

Grey Cloak scratched his name down on the paper. He

gave Sayma a sorrowful look. Her cheeks were wet with tears, and her shoulders heaved.

"Sayma, grab your belongings from your quarters, and see yourself out. You know where the exit is." Airius gave her a disappointed look. "I'd hate to have to notify the Honor Guard."

Sayma removed her apron and threw it at him. "I'll be gone before you know it!" She stormed out of the office. A clatter of broken glassware followed her departure.

Grey Cloak swallowed. *What was that all about? She didn't do anything. She was good.* He gave Airius a puzzled look.

"Don't look so long faced. We don't have a place for that here. Finish her assignments for the day, and tomorrow I want you to serve those on the castle tours."

Grey Cloak nodded. "Yes, Headmaster."

Airius grabbed the parchment, rolled it up, and stuck it in a drawer. "Off with you, then."

Grey Cloak hurried out of the office and after Sayma. He caught up with her down in the servants' quarters. She was coming down the hallway, with her things gathered in a leather satchel, her eyebrows knitted together and a stormy look in her eyes.

"Sayma, I'm sorry. I don't understand."

"Sure you don't. Get out of my way, job snatcher. This isn't the first time someone's tried to steal my position." She pushed past him. "Best of luck to you, Grey Cloak. I guess you got what you wanted."

"But I didn't want it. I just arrived." She moved up the stairs, and he hollered after her, "Go to the Tavern Dwellers Inn. Tell Aham I sent you. He'll take care of you."

Sayma was gone.

He kicked the wall. It had all happened so fast, and he was powerless to do anything about it. He might as well have been a fly on the wall. With his head down, he headed to his room and closed the door. His stomach felt like a giant pit.

This is awful. I like Sayma. She wasn't rigid like the others. Like Airius. Oh well, I'm not going to be here forever. I'll find her later, now I have to find Zora.

That was when Airius's orders hit him.

Did he say I'll be serving for the tours tomorrow? He stood up. *Zooks, yes!*

It was the break he needed. The tour ended at Codd's crypt.

Perfect! I'll be right where I need to be to steal Codd's shield.

He dropped to a knee and reached for his cloak where he'd placed it underneath his bed. His fingers came up empty. He flipped the bed over.

"Oh no, my cloak's gone!"

15

Dyphestive took two more hard licks from Hodges's jo stick to the side of the head.

Whack! Whack!

Hodges beat him like a drum for a few more seconds.

Dyphestive drew his legs up underneath himself and lunged at Hodges.

Hodges skipped away, but not before Dyphestive hammered the smaller man's shoulder. Hodges stumbled back and deftly caught his balance using his staff for support.

With a grunt, Dyphestive scrambled to his feet. He turned away from Hodges's next assault and blocked Hodges's jo stick with his own. The young fighters blasted away at each other, stick against stick.

The Honor Guards practically jumped out of their

boots, hooting and hollering. One wide-eyed man held the surging crowd back with his arms.

"Stay out of it! Stay out of it!" Sergeant Tinison screamed. "Let the inbreeds fight their own fight!"

Seconds into the match, it became very clear that Hodges could handle a jo stick like a master. He aimed for knuckles and cracked it against bone. Dyphestive held on and loosed a savage assault of his own. Using powerful strikes propelled by raw brawny muscle, he beat Hodges's twirling attacks aside. He struck harder and faster.

Clak! Clak! Clak!

Hodges spun away from Dyphestive's attacks, slipped past the bruising stick, and jabbed his stick into Dyphestive's ribs. Dyphestive let out a grunt, twisted at the hips, and whipped his stick flat into Hodges's back.

Whack!

Hodges's arms spread out, and he arched backward as if struck by lightning. He dropped flat to the ground just as a second attack swished over him. He rolled to the side, evading Dyphestive's heavy-handed blows. He cocked his knee back and kicked Dyphestive square in the nanoos.

The entire Honor Guard, including Dyphestive, doubled over and groaned. "Oooooooooooh!"

Dyphestive limped away, using his stick to prop himself up. His nostrils flared, and his blood ran red down his face. He squared off with Hodges and glared at the man, with fire in his eyes. He waved Hodges on. "Come on! Come on!"

He pointed to his skull and dropped his jo stick. "Take your best shot."

Many of the Honor Guards gasped.

One of them said, "He's crazy."

"I like crazy," said another.

"Bust the fool's melon open, Hodges! Teach him a lesson!"

Hodges jumped at the opportunity. Holding his jo stick high over his head, he brought it down with a wroth force on Dyphestive's skull.

Crack!

The jo stick broke on the brawny youth's head. It didn't leave a scratch.

The Honor Guard fell silent for a moment, then one of them said, "His skull is harder than Sarge's."

Hodges stepped backward, his face ashen.

Dyphestive snatched the other half of Hodges's staff from his hands and proceeded to beat him half to death until the Honor Guard finally pulled him off. His chest was heaving, and he lifted his eyes to the sky and let out a triumphant howl.

Sergeant Tinison wandered into the ring of stalwart men at a leisurely pace with his hands behind his back. "Well, well, well, look what we have left, a Beak and a Baby Face."

He eyeballed Dyphestive and the woman nicknamed Beak facing off in the middle. "It's been exciting. It's been very exciting, but now you're the last two, and we're only going to take one." He stopped and faced them. "You both have shown grit. I like it. You can fight. But let's change it up. Corporal, bring the buckets."

A clean-shaven pie-faced Honor Guard with a scar on his cheek brought over two wooden buckets. He set them upside down at Dyphestive's and Beak's feet. He checked for an approving look from Sergeant Tinison.

Sergeant Tinison shooed him away. "Get over there." He paced around the two competitors. "Stand on the buckets, donkey skulls."

Dyphestive stepped up on the round platform. His big boots hung over the edges. He glanced over at Beak. Her feet were much smaller, and she stood within the circle of the bucket's rim perfectly.

"Come on, Sarge, not the bucket test. Let them fight," one of the Honor Guard said. He was a long-limbed orc who stood half a head above the rest. "This is boring."

"How about all of you do the bucket test?" Sergeant Tinison shouted. "Would you like that? Or would you rather watch?"

The orc shrank away from his comrades' hot stares. "Did I say it was boring? I meant captivating." He offered a humble smile and clapped gently. "Very captivating."

Sergeant Tinison rolled his eyes and muttered under

his breath, "One orc spoils the whole bunch." He raised his jarring voice again. "Listen up, Beak and Baby Face. You're going to stand on those buckets in the hot sun all day or until one of you falls off. I bet you think that it sounds simple, but it's not. You're going to stand like a crane, one-legged. That's the rule. You stand on one leg, so pick your favorite." He glared at each of them. "Well, get a knee up, or I'll pick one for you!"

Dyphestive lifted his right knee. He spread out his hands and balanced himself.

Beak, who stood to his right, lifted her left knee.

"Outstanding!" Sergeant Tinison shouted at them. "Let's see which one of you tick turds wants this the most!" He turned on the Honor Guards. "What are you gawking at? We aren't going to watch them all day. We have work to do. Scatter, pigeons! Except you, Half-Wit. You stay with me." He pointed at the pie-faced soldier with a scar. "We'll keep an eye on them." He dabbed his sweaty forehead with a cloth. "Over there in the shade." He waddled off.

Dyphestive and Beak stood for hours without talking.

Beak broke the silence. "You might as well drop out," she said with the sun shining in her face. "I can do this all day."

"Huh," Dyphestive replied. "I can do this all day and all night."

She let out a pleasant but confident laugh. Aside from her crooked nose, Beak was an attractive young woman with refined features and long chestnut hair. "A big oaf like you might be able to beat a man with sticks, but I have the balance of a palace dancer. This challenge will be a breeze."

Dyphestive turned his head and started blowing at her.

"What are you doing?" she asked with an incredulous look.

"I'm trying to blow you over." He wobbled a bit, swung his arms, and regained his balance.

"You really aren't very good at this." She offered her hand. "My name isn't Beak, even though it's fitting. I'm Shannon."

He accepted her firm grip. "Nice to meet you, Shannon. I'm Dyphestive."

"Interesting name."

"How come you want to become an Honor Guard?" he asked.

"My father was a Monarch Knight. I'm going to be one too. This isn't my first crack at the Honor Guard either. It's the fifth and my last chance to make it." She stood as still and composed as a post. "I'm not going to lose."

"A shame because I don't intend to lose either." He decided to get into her head. "And I never lose, but it sounds to me like you've lost four times so far. That doesn't sound good for you. It sounds like you're better at that than winning."

"We'll see."

"You said your father was a Monarch Knight?" he asked. "What happened?"

"He died not so long ago."

"Oh, I'm sorry to hear that. My sorrows." He wobbled again and regained his balance.

"Don't fall off, Baby Face!" Sergeant Tinison hollered. "Or you'll crack the courtyard!"

"Did he die in combat? What was his name, if you don't mind me asking?"

"Yes." Her eyes narrowed and focused on the courtyard wall in front of them. "His name was Adanadel. The Doom Riders killed him."

Dyphestive's heart jumped. *Adanadel!*

Beak finished with a heated stare, "And I'm going to avenge him."

16

"So much for slipping in and out," Jakoby said as he drew his sword.

The faceless warriors pulled curved blades from the folds of their crimson robes and slowly advanced down the steps. Behind them, at the top of the stairs, the wizard Finton Slay looked on with a crimson glow in his haunting eyes.

"I hope you're really good with that thing," Than said, nodding to Jakoby's longsword.

Jakoby's sword had been made in the Monarch Knights' forges and blessed by their enchanters. Its straight two-edged blade was razor-sharp, and the sword guard had crowns on the end. It was a work of beauty.

As the Iron Devils advanced, the lizardmen guards crept in from the other side with studded clubs in hand.

Jakoby, Than, and Leena formed a circle back-to-back. Leena whipped out two pairs of nunchakus.

"She really likes those little sticks, doesn't she?" Than commented.

Jakoby held his sword in front of his chest and closed his eyes. "Yes," he said, "but not as much as I love my sword. Watch yourself, Than. I'm about to unleash steel wind on these vermin." He channeled the energy of a sword saint, turning his blood to fire. Energy spread from the pureness of his heart and pumped into the rest of his body. His longsword shimmered, and he opened his eyes and attacked.

WITH A DETERMINED LOOK in her eyes, long-haired Leena stepped toward the lizardmen, twirling both pairs of nunchakus.

The savage expressions of the lizardmen almost turned to laughter as they watched the spinning sticks. They were monsters compared to Leena, with bulging muscle underneath their scales. A lizardman with gummy eyes slapped another in the chest, hissing a chuckle.

Leena whipped the nunchakus faster. The spinning halves of the ebony sticks ignited with mystic cherry-red fire. The weapons spoke to the wind.

Whiiiiiirrrrr!

The lizardmen's slanted eyes widened, and their jaws dropped.

The nunchakus flicked out like lightning. In a split moment, the nunchakus in Leena's right hand clobbered a lizardman in the jaw so hard it spun him around.

Pow!

Her left set struck another lizardman in the shoulder with explosive force.

Kapow!

The cherry fire of the nunchakus formed shields of bright energy. They cracked knees and busted bones.

Pow! Kapow!

Leena attacked the brawny guards like a swarm of stinging hornets. The fire of her nunchakus sent them flying backward.

Kapow! Pow!

The gummy-eyed lizardman snuck in behind her. She back-kicked him in the groin, spun around, and clobbered him like a drummer doing a solo.

Nocka-nocka-nocka-nocka-pow!

Using her blazing speed and skills, she beat the scales off the inferior lizardmen. The brutes sprawled on the stone floor, knocked out or licking their wounds. That was when the four-armed ogre crept in behind her and scooped her up in his massive arms.

THE IRON DEVILS' body language told it all. They moved with the subtle ease of assassins and night prowlers. Silently, they descended the steps as one, their stares icy behind their iron masks.

Assassins! Jakoby lunged at the nearest assassin. He pierced the man's chest and killed him with a lethal strike. *I hate assassins.*

Two more assassins flanked him and struck. Jakoby anticipated the maneuver and dove to the ground to avoid their strike. The assassins gored one another and collapsed. Jakoby aided their descent, cutting one assassin's leg off at the knee. He spun on his back like a turtle and chopped through the other one's ankle.

Three down, three to go!

He had focus. Strength. Speed. He had it all.

An Iron Devil jumped from higher up the stairs, his robes billowing as he seemed to float through the air.

Jakoby deflected the strike and countered with his own. He split open the assassin's mask. Metal sank into solid bone. The mask fell away from the assassin's face, revealing a skull with decaying muscle and flesh hanging off it. Its burning blue eyes dimmed.

"Ghouls! I should have known, with a wizard involved. Don't let them touch you, Leena!"

The ghouls were men hovering between life and death. They were servants of the dark arts, who killed and fed off the living. Jakoby stepped up his game. A part of him held back when it came to killing men, but when it came to the arcane abominations of the world, he didn't hold back.

Four down, only two to go!

Two of the undead assassins came at him, their steel spinning. They struck with supernatural strength and speed.

He parried one blade and boot-kicked another assassin in the gut. He gored another assassin in the belly and let him slide off his blade. The faceless assassin that he cut through the knee grabbed his legs. Its ice-blue eyes were burning again. It opened its jaws and bit him. "Get off me, fiend!" Jakoby screamed as he hacked into it.

All the Iron Devils that had fallen by his blade were coming at him again. If they couldn't walk, they crawled. They would not die.

Finton Slay cackled with glee. "What's the matter? Can't you kill them? Hah-hah-hah-hah-hah!"

Jakoby's sword rose up and down. It ripped through robes and dry bones and flesh. Even the Iron Devils' severed appendages crawled at him. Fingers flexed and stretched and scurried across the floor. He stabbed a loose hand he'd severed and flung it away. The Iron Devils— hacked up with hunks and bits missing—clawed at him and kept coming. Their strong fingers and teeth locked onto his robes and started to drag him down. "Nooooo!" he shouted. He stabbed downward again and again. "Noooooo!" The swarm of darkness was taking him.

THE FOUR-ARMED OGRE squeezed Leena so hard that her shoulder popped. Her eyes bugged out, and she couldn't catch her breath. She threw her head back with all her might, busting the back of her head on the ogre's rock-hard chin.

The ogre moaned with triumph as the glow of her nunchakus faded. It squeezed harder.

Leena's eyes bugged out of her head. The nunchakus slipped from her fingers and clattered onto the stone floor. The ogre crushed her body like a vise. Her ribs cracked. She kicked and squirmed as her eyes rolled up into her head, and she let out a final painful breath.

17

"No-no-no-no," Grey Cloak cried under his breath as he turned his quarters upside down. The Cloak of Legends was nowhere to be found. He'd looked under his bed and mattress as well as the one beside it. He'd looked in the wooden footlocker too. It had vanished. He balled his fists and screamed inside himself.

EEEEEEYAAAARGH!

He made a quick trip to the other servants' quarters and searched them high and low. The only person he thought could have taken it was Sayma.

She must have done it to spite me, but why? I didn't wrong her. Airius did! He snapped his fingers. *Wait! I can catch her.*

Grey Cloak barreled down the servants' hall and headed up the stairs. Airius stood at the top of the steps and was on his way down. With his hands on his hips, he said, "Why aren't you upstairs working? Do I have to release you before you've even started?"

"No, I..."

Arius eyed him suspiciously. "I what? Let me guess. You're going after Sayma. Well, so you know, she's cleared the moat."

"But—"

Airius hooked his arm before he could pass. "What is this about, Grey Cloak? Hmmm?" he droned. "You are flummoxed. I can't have you flummoxed in front of the Monarchs. Tell me. A little honesty can go a long way with me."

Grey Cloak's fingers needled the palm of his hand. With his chin down, he admitted, "I lost something. I thought Sayma might have taken it."

"I see." Airius stepped aside, and with a snap of his hand, the Cloak of Legends hung suspended in front of him. "Is this the item you're looking for?"

"Yes," Grey Cloak said with a sigh of relief. He reached for it.

Airius pulled it away. "This garment belongs in your footlocker, not underneath your mattress. If I had a silver chip for every time I found a servant squirreling away something below their mattress, I'd be a Monarch." He rubbed the cloak between his thumb and fingers. "It's of a remarkable quality for an unremarkable cloak. Where did you come by it?"

Grey Cloak rubbed the back of his head. "Uh... Red Cliff. I bought it there some time ago."

Airius shoved it against Grey Cloak's chest. "There is a peg on the back of your quarters door. Use it. Put that rag away, and get to work."

"Right away," Grey Cloak said, as he took several steps at a time.

"Youths," Airius said smugly as he turned away. "They are so attached to the silliest things."

Grey Cloak paid him no mind.

Yes! Yes! Yes! I have it! Zora, I'm coming to get you!

"WHAT'S THE MATTER WITH YOU?" Beak tilted her head. "You look like you swallowed a bug."

"No, I-I lost my train of thought," Dyphestive replied. "What were we talking about?"

"My father. Thunderbolts, you're as bright as a bug bear, aren't you?"

"I wish," he said. He caught her smiling. "I didn't mean to pry about your father. I hope I didn't stir up too much."

"I'm always stirred up."

He didn't reply. *Bend my horseshoes! I can't believe Adanadel is her father.* The sinking feeling in his gut quickly became worse. He hadn't thought about Adanadel in a long time. The former Monarch Knight had recruited him and

Grey Cloak into Talon. Their adventures had been short-lived. When the Doom Riders had arrived in Raven Cliff, Adanadel had died at their hands while trying to rescue Dyphestive.

This is awful. Should I tell her or not?

The wooden bucket groaned underneath him as if a heavy weight had landed on his shoulders. The shame of being a Doom Rider assailed him, and his guilt grew.

"Are you well? Now you look green, and you're sweating awfully bad," she said.

"It must be the sun, I guess. I can't take the heat."

"We haven't been out here that long. You aren't going to quit, are you?"

Flashes of all the horrible things he'd done as a Doom Rider filled his head as a flood of terrible memories came back.

Focus, I need to be here. I need to be here for Zora. He gave Beak a nervous glance. *I can't believe she's Adanadel's daughter. It's my fault her father died. I can't take this away from her too.*

Dyphestive wobbled. He was about to let himself slip off. The wooden bucket gave way under his great weight.

"Bloody biscuits, Baby Face! You owe me a bucket!" Sergeant Tinison said. He and Half-Wit hustled over to Dyphestive.

Half-Wit scratched his head. "If the bucket breaks, who wins?"

"Beak wins," Sergeant Tinison stated.

Dyphestive's competitive fire flared, and he shot back, "I'm still standing on one leg. It's not my fault the bucket broke."

"It is your fault anvi-arse," Sergeant Tinison retorted.

Honor Guards broke away from their duties and gathered around. "What's going on?"

"Baby Face broke his bucket, so Beak wins."

The Honor Guards murmured amongst themselves.

"That hardly seems fair."

"They should do it again."

"How is it his fault the bucket broke?"

"Gum up!" Sergeant Tinison said. "We can only take one!"

"Says who?" Half-Wit asked.

Sergeant Tinison got in Half-Wit's face. "Are you challenging my authority?"

Half-Wit stammered, "Y-yes, Sarge!"

"What about the rest of you?" Sergeant Tinison argued. "Are you challenging my decision too?"

"We're all Honor Guard," the long-limbed orc said. "I think we should put it to a vote."

"Well, I'm so glad that Long Neck has something to say. Say, Long Neck, after you finish voting, you can clean the squalor stalls for a month. How does that sound? Huh? Huh? Huh?" Sergeant Tinison asked.

Long Neck crossed his arms. "If it means righting a wrong, I'm behind it."

"Fine, you bunch of slack-jawed ninnies. We'll put it to a vote, then! It has to be unanimous too!" Sergeant Tinison glanced at Dyphestive and Beak. "Will you put your feet down? You look like you belong in a cornfield." He faced his men. "By a show of hands, who wants Beak?"

No one lifted their hand.

Beak's chin dropped.

"I see, I see," Sergeant Tinison muttered. He lifted his glass-breaking voice. "And who wants Dyphestive to stay?"

The soldiers' hands remained at their sides.

Sergeant Tinison grinned. "Who wants both?"

Every Honor Guard lifted their hands high.

Sergeant Tinison casually lifted his. He turned on his heel and addressed Dyphestive and Beak. "Welcome to the Honor Guard."

Beak jumped into Dyphestive's arms and wrapped her limbs around him. "Yes!" Noticing all eyes on her, she quickly jumped away and said to Sergeant Tinison, "Sorry, sir."

"Heh, don't do it again. Honor Guard, what do we say?" He cupped his hand to his ear.

"Long live the monarchy!"

"I can't heeeeaaaaar yoooouuuuuu!"

"LONG LIVE THE MONARCHY!"

Sergeant Tinison saluted his men. "See these donkey

skulls to their quarters, and go to the galley and get some chow." He eyed them. "What are you waiting for? Move it! Move it! Move it!"

Dyphestive bounded after the others, with his heart racing. He was a novice in the Honor Guard. It meant something. Sergeant Tinison hooked his arm as he passed. "Sir?"

"I'm going to be watching you, Baby Face, because something tells me there's more to you than I see. I hope you don't disappoint me."

"I won't, sir. I won't."

Sergeant Tinison stuck out his chin and nodded. Under his breath, he said, "We'll see about that, won't we?"

18

The four-armed ogre finished squishing Leena and dropped her limp body to the floor. The hairy eight-footer with a bulging belly squatted over the monk. He nudged her with his fingers and tilted his head.

With the ogre's fetid breath in her face, she opened her eyes. The ogre let out a surprised grunt. Leena sprang up and heel-kicked the ogre in the beans five times in rapid succession. With a groan, the ogre dropped his hands over his crotch.

Leena snatched up one of her nunchakus with her good arm and clocked the ogre in the throat. Her small sticks spun with wildfire, and she battered his thick skull. He tried to cover up his head and took a shot to the knee.

Whackatahkrak!

The ogre flailed wildly, trying to smash the woman.

She busted his elbows and wrists. A quick and mighty strike cracked his nose. She spun around and roundhouse kicked him in the groin. The furious ogre beat his chest with four mighty fists, howled at the top of his lungs, and ran like a huge ape to cower inside his den.

Leena set her eyes on Jakoby just as the Iron Devils dragged him down. She dashed his way, her dislocated shoulder hanging limp. She hit the fiends with everything she had. Than stood in the knot of the unliving, pulling them away.

Finton Slay cackled with triumphant laughter. "Die, fools! Die!"

Than ripped a ghoul's skull from its narrow shoulders and hurled it at Finton Slay. The skull caught the bony man square in the chest and knocked him backward. Than ripped his legs away from an Iron Devil and charged the stairs. "Nogard! Nogard!"

Jakoby spun his sword in and out of the attackers' bodies. They started to pile up at his feet. He brought his sword down with two hands on a ghoul that lost its life. "The harvest is ripe!"

Right by his side, Leena blasted away with her nunchakus. The fiends would fall then climb up again with broken jaws, knees, and elbows, giving them a staggered gait.

With a twist of his hips, Jakoby cleared a ghoul's head

from its shoulders. "There's no coming back from that!" Up and down his sword went, tearing one down then another.

Leena watched the last one fall with the final spin of her whirling stick. She hit the ghoul so hard, its face exploded. Bone chips and dead skin went flying.

"Up here!" Than hollered. He had Finton Slay in a headlock.

Leena's and Jakoby's clothing was torn to shreds. They had cuts, scrapes, and bite marks all over as they ambled up the stairs.

"You're looking for Zora, aren't you?" Finton Slay asked.

"No, we're looking for the nearest necromancer. Oh, it looks like we found one," Jakoby said. He suddenly grimaced, and his sword arm shook.

"What's the matter? Feeling rigid? Is your blood turning cold? Soon you will be one of those Devils—*urk!*"

Leena groin kicked Finton Slay.

"You little witch, I'll fry you after your bones turn brittle."

Than cranked up the pressure. "Where is Zora, you little worm?"

"You have more important matters to worry about, it seems. At least Zora is still among the living. They are not." Finton Slay's body collapsed into smoke, his head drifting away last, saying, "Goodbye, fools. Don't forget the shield." His body vaporized and was gone.

Than stood with his jaw hanging and his arms empty. "I hate it when that happens."

Jakoby and Leena collapsed on the floor, their faces turning ashen.

"So cold." Jakoby's teeth chattered. "My bones are freezing. My breath is frosty. I don't want to die like this."

Than kneeled between the two of them and locked his strong hands on their wrists. "You won't." His hands radiated with quavering golden light. His eyes shone like the sun.

Leena and Jakoby gasped as if taking a breath for the first time. Their wounds healed. Leena pushed herself to her feet, bowed to Than, walked to a wall, and shoved her shoulder against it. The shoulder popped into place. Her eyes didn't even water.

Jakoby offered his hand, and Than hauled him to his feet. "Thanks, my friend. I owe you my life."

"Save it for someone else." Than staggered. His jaws and cheeks looked more sunken than before. He swayed.

Jakoby caught him by the waist. "What's wrong?"

"Nothing," Than grunted as he straightened. "At least we know where Zora isn't, but they're onto us. We better go. It's up to Grey Cloak and Dyphestive now." He eyed the prisoners' arms stretching out past the bars. "But let's free more prisoners first."

19

After performing his daily duties, Grey Cloak tracked down Dyphestive at the Honor Guard barracks. It was there that he ran into Captain Cleotus, who was talking to Sergeant Tinison. They were smoking curled pipes made from elk horn.

"Ah, it's Grey Cloak. It looks like you survived your first day with Airius," Captain Cleotus said with amusement. "Let me guess. You want to see your blood brother."

"If possible, Captain."

"It's not my call. He's a novice with the Honor Guard now. Allow me to introduce you to Sergeant Tinison."

"Nice to meet you—"

"Stifle it. Can't you see I'm smoking?" Sergeant Tinison spewed a stream of yellow smoke. "He's in there somewhere." He hitched his thumb toward the open door.

"Thank you." Grey Cloak started to duck inside, when Captain Cleotus placed a hand on his shoulder. "I hear you'll be serving on the tours tomorrow."

"The tours." Sergeant Tinison rolled his eyes. "Waste of resources."

"Anyway, I look forward to seeing you in action. Not so much as your brother. It seems that his first day was quite impressive. *Quite* impressive."

"It does me good to hear it." Grey Cloak nodded and headed into the barracks. Inside were rows of single beds with footlockers in front of them. It was much like the servants' quarters but more military-like and filled with stout men and women, mostly men, wearing their evening shirts and britches. He caught a glimpse of Dyphestive lying down on a cot at the very end. Waving his hand, he caught his brother's eye.

Dyphestive sat up and smiled. He waved his brother to the back, but Grey Cloak shook his head. He didn't feel comfortable wandering among all the soldiers who didn't know him. He preferred to use more discretion.

Dyphestive got up and met him at the barracks' entrance. "How did your day go?"

"It could have been better. Yours?"

"Great!"

"Is there somewhere we can talk in private?"

"There's a garden in the back that the Honor Guard keeps up. Follow me." Dyphestive led them to the backside of the barracks and through a door into a fairly large vegetable and floral garden. Stone benches lined a stone walkway that surrounded the separate gardens. They took a seat farthest from the barracks while still facing it.

Dyphestive quickly started talking about his day with the giddiness of a five-year-old, maintaining one long run-on sentence.

When Grey Cloak realized that his brother wasn't going to stop, he cut him off. "Enough, enough, I get it," Grey Cloak said, trying to be polite. "Honestly, I didn't think you would embrace it so much."

"I love it! I've been talking to the other guards, and they said if I complete the training and become Honor Guard, I can work as a knight's squire then become a Monarch Knight, like Codd."

Grey Cloak's head dropped. "What are you talking about? We're here to find a way to save Zora. I'm going to need your help."

Dyphestive frowned. "I know, but—"

"But nothing, we are here for one reason." He pulled Dyphestive's chin toward him and looked him in the eye. "We have to save Zora. Our friend."

"They're going to swear me in tomorrow. I can't break my word."

"Don't do it. Quit."

"I like it."

Grey Cloak tapped his heel. He had no idea what was

happening to his brother, but it seemed that Grey Cloak was losing him. He didn't like it. "What about your oath to me? We're blood brothers."

Dyphestive's broad shoulders deflated. Sadly, he said, "I know." He sighed. "I really like this though."

In all their lives, Dyphestive had never asked for or wanted anything. Now it seemed he'd found something he wanted. He seemed determined to be a Monarch Knight for some crazy reason.

With the crickets chirping and a gentle wind rustling the fragrant flowered vines and bushes, Grey Cloak sat silently by his brother in what had suddenly become a glum evening. With sadness in his heart, he said, "The entire reason we left Dark Mountain was to be free to become whatever we wanted to be. I always thought whatever it was, we'd be together. If becoming a Monarch Knight is what you want, I want you to know that I support you." He patted his brother's back. "I'm sure Zora will understand too."

"I'm sorry. I didn't really think I'd like it that much. I don't know why, but I do. It feels right. And Sergeant Tinison, he's really funny. He doesn't mean to be, but he is. But I can't laugh out loud about it. Everyone else does behind his back." He squirmed in his seat. "There's another thing. I made a friend of sorts."

"I imagine you did."

"No, she's different. Her name's Beak, well, Shannon actually. Everyone has a nickname. I'm Baby Face."

Grey Cloak picked a flower from the garden and started plucking the petals off. "It sounds a lot more pleasant than Iron Bones. I was actually fond of that one."

"Funny that you mention it. Beak is Adanadel's daughter."

Grey Cloak sat up. "What?" A light went on in his head. "Ah, that's why you want to stay. You feel guilty, don't you?"

"No. Yes. Well, it's not why I want to stay, but I need to tell her what happened and why. She doesn't know, Grey. She deserves to know."

"Tell her after we save Zora."

Dyphestive shook his head. "I can't." He fished the flying potion out of his pocket. "Take this. I won't need it."

Grey Cloak stood up. "No, you keep it as something to remember me by. Goodbye, blood brother." He stormed away.

20

Grey Cloak sat inside his quarters, brooding.

How could he do this to me? To me? I have one day left to save Zora, and he's going to abandon me? Ridiculous!

He lay flat on his back, tossing an acorn-sized flashing in the air and catching it. As aggravated as he was, he envisioned exactly what he was going to do.

You can do this, Grey Cloak. You can do it. All alone. I'll take my chances.

He'd been up all night. He tried to sleep, which he never did much of, and he tossed and turned when he succeeded. He was torn between being hurt and angry, wrestling with whether or not that was it for him and Dyphestive. They'd been through so much together. Dyphestive had been as loyal as a hound.

Did I do something wrong?

He blamed it on the Doom Riders. They'd changed Dyphestive when they'd manipulated his mind. He hadn't been the same since.

Outside the door of his quarters, he heard the soft footsteps of the servants shuffling by. It was the wee hours of the morning, before the monarchy woke, and the servants were preparing the morning meal.

He rolled off his bed and kneeled by his footlocker.

It's time.

He pulled out his servant's clothing, dressed, and loaded his pockets with the slender potion vials and flashings. He pressed his hands over his clothing to make sure they were well concealed.

Airius doesn't miss anything. I have to be careful.

He lifted the Cloak of Legends out of the footlocker by its shoulders. He felt naked when he didn't wear it, and it had been over a day. "I wish I could take you with me. Don't you go anywhere." He folded it neatly inside the footlocker, as opposed to hanging it on the door peg, and closed the lid. He patted himself down once more and exited his quarters.

I can do this. Even without help. I'll take my chances.

Codd's domed crypt was half-full of excited observers. Captain Cleotus gallantly shared the heroic exploits of Codd, the father of the Monarch Knights. It was the first tour of the day, and Grey Cloak's palms hadn't stopped tingling. As he and his crew of servants served the tour, he made a mental note of every detail of the crypt.

Nothing had changed since he took the tour two days ago aside from the new tour guests. Surrounding the ominous and imposing figure of Codd were the twelve outer columns. In between those columns were twelve statues of knights, with Honor Guards in full armor beside them. The Honor Guard stood as still as fence posts, not blinking. They wore round open-faced helms, and one of them was Dyphestive.

Grey Cloak didn't make eye contact with his brother.

He'll probably turn me in.

Between serving the tour delicacies that the children couldn't keep their grubby fingers out of, Grey Cloak stole glances at the yonders lurking at the tops of the columns. He'd counted twelve of the winged eyeballs in all. They had fastened themselves to the marble pillars and blended in like fixtures, but he could still see the whites of their eyes.

He nonchalantly patted the flashings in his pocket.

This better work. It has to work.

He was putting his faith in Batram's words and hoping he got it right. He only had one shot, and if he failed, he would probably be locked in the Monarchs' dungeons for a lifetime or quickly fed to the moat monsters.

Focus. Focus. Focus.

Captain Cleotus was only a few minutes away from winding up his spiel about Codd.

Grey Cloak's heart started to race. He could try to steal the shield on the next tour and do more planning. He shook off the doubt.

I'll take my chances.

After one last look at Codd and the shield, he locked the image in his mind. The flashings were powerful enough to temporarily blind a person. He felt bad for the children. It might scare them, but at least no one would get hurt. As for Codd's shield, he didn't think of it as stealing so much as borrowing it. After he freed Zora, he planned to put it back or at least let the Monarchs know who really stole it. Perhaps they would understand.

Grey Cloak fished three flashings out of his pocket. With his back to the columns, he casually dropped one flashing to the floor and squeezed his eyes shut.

Booomph!

The blinding flash was so bright that he could see the veins on the insides of his eyelids. The tour erupted in screams.

Captain Cleotus barked orders. "Attack. We're under attack!"

Grey Cloak set down his tray and moved toward Codd's pedestal. Everyone fumbled and stumbled over the floor. The yonders dropped from their perches. As fast as a cat, Grey Cloak crawled up beside Codd's massive oval shield while everyone fought to regain their senses.

"I can't see!" members of the tour cried.

"I'm blind!" the children screamed.

As the sea of commotion built up in the crypt, Grey Cloak grabbed his shrinking potion. He knew it was meant for consumption, but he decided to take a risk and try something different. He tore off the cork and poured the swirling orange contents onto the shield. Nothing happened. *Zooks!*

"No one move!" Captain Cleotus shouted. "Be still! Don't panic! Can anyone see?"

The people replied with a bunch of mumbling and groaned nos. Many of the people sounded like they were about to die.

"Castle Monarch is under attack!" one woman screamed.

"Black Frost comes to put us to sleep!" said another.

Grey Cloak noticed some of the yonders rising up from the floor and flying erratically.

One of the soldiers said, "I think I can see, Captain."

Grey Cloak closed his eyes and kept his head down. He busted another flashing on the ground.

Booomph!

The crypt erupted in earsplitting screams.

Grey Cloak opened his eyes. The shield still hadn't shrunk.

Bloody horseshoes! What do I do?

21

Grey Cloak dumped the rest of the potion on the shield. The orange liquid dripped around the six-foot-tall oval shield's rim. In the meantime, he tried to pry the shield away from Codd's iron grasp. It didn't budge.

"Honor Guard! Man your positions!" Captain Cleotus stumbled through the crowd. "Everyone on the tour, breathe easy. There is no danger here. The Honor Guard will protect you!"

"We are doomed! Doomed!" a woman cried out as she huddled over her children. "The Monarchs have been slain!"

"No one has been slain!" Captain Cleotus rubbed his eyes. "I assure you. This is only a mishap—ulp!" He tripped over a member of the tour and fell to the ground.

"The captain's dead!" the same woman shouted.

"I'm fine! I only fell! Thunderbolts, quit your crowing, woman!"

The yonders started to rise again and fluttered like moths through the crypt. Grey Cloak used his last flashing.

Booomph!

When he opened his eyes, the yonders clinging to the walls and columns were dropping like flies. He reached for the shield. It wasn't there. It had shrunk to the size of a medallion he could fit between his thumb and finger. Its tiny straps were pinched between Codd's knuckles.

Sweet Gapoli!

He pried the shield away and stuffed it into his pocket. As the grumbling crowd came round, he made his way back to his serving tray. He took out the shield, wrapped it in a cloth napkin, and set it on the serving platter.

Now it's time to sell it.

Over the next several moments, the crowd and soldiers calmed down. They all rubbed their eyes and blinked. Grey Cloak helped many of them to their feet.

"Is everyone all right?" Captain Cleotus asked. His pupils were huge, the same as everyone else's. "What in the blazing furnaces happened? No one leaves the crypt until I get it sorted out. No one!"

Propelled by their creepy bat wings, the yonders rose into the air. Their staggered flight patterns steadied, and they whizzed around the people like a swarm of hornets. Grey Cloak found himself eyes to eyeball with a yonder that floated right in front of him. He feigned dizziness, and it flew away. The yonders combed the entire room, exhaustively searching every person, place, and thing. Suddenly they swirled around Codd like a hive of angry bees.

Captain Cleotus stood beside Grey Cloak, scratching his head. "I wonder what that's all about." His eyes widened. "Burning cornstalks! The shield is missing! Honor Guard! Nobody leaves this room. I mean no one! I want every person, every nook and cranny searched." He caught Dyphestive's eye as he was standing near the exit. "Close that door now! Half-Wit, make sure every tour member, servant, and soldier is accounted for."

In military fashion, the Honor Guard thoroughly patted every person down, including one another. Grey Cloak stood by his serving tray, not moving. He put his hands up while a comely woman Honor Guard searched him.

"I haven't seen you before," she said.

"I'm new. Airius brought me in yesterday."

She patted his backside and whispered in his ear, "I hope you stay around. Go stay over there with the others who have been searched."

"Can I grab my tray? Uh, I didn't catch your name."

"Olive." She squatted down and picked through the platter of desserts. She even lifted the cloth napkin with the shield inside it, tapped it in her palm, and set it down. "Take it away, handsome."

"Olive, cut the chitter-chatter," Captain Cleotus said. "Did anyone see anything?"

"All I saw was a bright flash, three times," a gusty half-orc woman said. She was as big as the captain and wore her hair in multiple black braids. She had two children with her. "I still have huge spots in my eyes. I say a wizard snatched it. Zapped in and zapped out. And I want a reimbursement for my tour. All of it!"

"Don't make me tell you to gum up again. Do you hear? No one goes anywhere until that shield is found."

The half-orc woman looked around the crypt. "That shield's bigger than me. It's impossible for anyone to hide it. Lords of thunder, let's go. I'm getting hungry."

There was a distinct knock on the door.

Captain Cleotus approached the door and said to Dyphestive, "Open it." When the door parted, he briefly stepped outside and had words with somebody. When he came back in, his face was ashen. He cleared his throat and spoke up. "If I can have your attention, everyone. All members of the tour will be seen out. The rest of us stay."

The tour was escorted through the doors, and Captain Cleotus closed the door behind them.

He stood before the men and women in the room while the yonders hovered over them. "Codd's shield is gone. I alone am to blame." He took off his sword belt and dropped it to the floor. "I've been stripped of my rank and have been asked to leave the premises immediately. I want to say that it's been a pleasure to serve the Honor Guard. Long live the monarchy."

The yonders surrounded Captain Cleotus and swirled around him like a tornado. They moved so quickly the captain was blurred from sight as they created an eerie whistle of wind.

Grey Cloak covered his ears. He wasn't the only one.

The yonders slowed, and Captain Cleotus had disappeared. Only his armor and gear remained.

With his arm hairs standing on end, Grey Cloak caught Dyphestive's shocked and disappointed look. He glanced away.

It's not my fault.

22

———

After the crypt investigation was over, Grey Cloak was sent back to his quarters and told to wait. He quickly closed the door and grabbed his cloak.

It's time to move on. I don't know how long this shrinking potion will last.

He'd been sweating sling bullets ever since the investigation began. According to the Honor Guard, the Monarchs wanted to interview everyone individually. *There's no way the potion will last so long.*

Grey Cloak's inner hourglass was draining. He moved with urgency, knowing that at any moment the shield could enlarge again. He had no idea how long it would last, but he'd made it this far. Now, he had to find a way to depart unnoticed.

He tucked the shrunken shield into the back of his pants. *I can't put it inside my cloak pocket, or it will get trapped.*

He opened the door to his quarters and looked down both sides of the hallway. The way was clear. He headed out. Up in the kitchens, the servants buzzed with gossip. Grey Cloak evaded their prying eyes and aimed for the back exit that led to the courtyard gardens. From there, he would blend in with the tour that might not have exited yet or possibly latch onto one of the dignitaries being herded out.

At the threshold of the back exit, Airius stepped in front of him. "Where do you think you're going? The Honor Guard hasn't released anyone as far as I'm aware." He fingered the Cloak of Legends. "And what are you doing with this?"

Thinking on his feet, Grey Cloak replied, "After today, I don't think that I want to be a servant. I'm shaken up. I'm not fit for this."

"Don't be silly." Airius nudged him back inside the kitchen. "From what I heard, you handled yourself quite well. Go back to your quarters, and we can talk about it later."

"I really don't want to. I'm sorry."

"No one is leaving without the Monarchs' express permission. Believe me when I say that you aren't going anywhere." Airius grabbed his shoulders and started to turn him. "Wait in your room."

The shield bulged in the back of Grey Cloak's pants. He could feel it suddenly growing. "Oh my!" He faced Airius as he pulled the shield from his backside. "I really have to go."

Airius raised an eyebrow. "What's wrong with you? You look sick. Are you unwell?"

Grey Cloak concealed the shield behind his back. It was growing in his hands. He smirked guiltily. "I'm feeling well enough, but I'm not so certain about you." The shield grew so big, his arms could no longer contain it. Its great size covered him like a shell.

Airius's eyes widened. "Th-th-the shield?"

"Sorry, Airius." Grey Cloak clobbered the elf in the jaw. "That's for Sayma." He glanced behind him. The kitchen was a commotion of jabbering servants not paying attention. He hauled Airius's limp body into a pantry and closed the elf inside. Just before he departed, he said, "Have shield, will travel."

The kitchen was located at the back end of the castle's front entrance. The castle wall was only thirty yards away, with a vegetable garden containing rows of cornstalks in between. Grey Cloak slipped into the corn rows and hunkered down. *So close, but how am I going to get beyond that wall?*

As far as he knew, the only way in or out was Monarch Castle's main drawbridge. He didn't have time to find another way. He eyed Cod's shield. It was a beautiful oval shield with an elegant sunburst pattern on the front and two leather straps behind it. It was easily big enough for him to hide completely behind.

Hmmm... it would make an excellent canoe. I wonder if it would float.

He ducked through the corn rows near the edge and looked skyward. Honor Guard manned the top of the castle wall and the towers sitting forty yards apart. Many of the guards leaned over the edge, looking down on the court-yards. They were spread out along the wall as far as the eye could see, and they weren't alone either. The Monarch Knights, in brilliant full plate armor, stood among them, shouting commands with authoritative voices.

I'm never going to make it out that way.

He noticed huge storm drains that sloped away from the castle and dipped out of sight underneath the wall. Leaving the shield behind, he stole over to a drain and crept close to the wall. A grid of metal bars blocked his passage, but they looked wide enough for him to squeeze through.

I might make it, but not with the shield.

With time running out, he moved back into the small cornfield to come up with another plan. He spied a small wagon at the end of the garden. He pulled the wagon to the edge of the corn rows, covered the shield with his cloak, and wary of the soldiers on the wall, he loaded it quickly into the wagon. From there, he nonchalantly rolled up his white sleeves and loaded the wagon with stalks of corn.

Once the wagon was half-full, he pulled it by the handle toward the front gate.

A horrible plan, but I'll take my chances.

He kept his head down and whistled a cheerful tune, and no one paid him any mind. As he traveled closer to the drawbridge gate, he noticed that the portcullis was closed.

Now what? Shall I abandon the wagon and return later? I'm so close. All I need is a way past the gate.

The Honor Guards at the wall entrance waved him over. He lifted his head and eyed them. Dyphestive stood among them in a full scale-armor uniform with the yellow sash of a novice.

Zooks. There's no turning back now.

23

"What is one of Airius's servants doing all the way over here?" a gusty Honor Guard asked. Grey Cloak recognized him as Sergeant Tinison, who Captain Cleotus had introduced to Grey Cloak the night before. "No one comes or goes. Weren't you supposed to be confined to your quarters?"

"I've been cleared," Grey Cloak said. Thinking on his feet, he added, "Airius told me to gather food to take to the cathedral to give to the needy. But I must admit, he seemed very distracted."

"You think, Big Ears?" Sergeant Tinison scoffed. "We've got a heap of woes on our shoulders, and Airius wants to feed the needy? If it were me, I'd toss all those vagrants in the moat." He grumbled curses under his breath. "Lazy alley trolls."

"I'll take the wagon back if you wish, Sergeant, or I can wait until the commotion is over," he offered.

Sergeant Tinison plucked an ear of corn out of the wagon. "I hate corn, but I wouldn't feed it to street dung either. Take it back to the garden until the smoke clears. If it ever does. Thunderbolts! Someone's probably going to get the guillotine if that shield isn't found." His eyes slid over to Dyphestive and the young woman with a crooked nose standing beside them. "Baby Face and Beak, first assignment, search that wagon and get it out of here."

"Aye, Sergeant!" Beak said as she snapped her heels together.

Dyphestive followed suit. "Aye, Sergeant."

Perfect, the fortune I needed.

Grey Cloak dared a look at his brother and shrugged his eyebrows. Dyphestive glared at him. He tilted his head toward the wagon to silently say, "Get on with it before she does."

Dyphestive moved to the back of the wagon and muscled his way in beside Beak. "I'll do this."

"What do you mean, you'll do this?" she exclaimed. "I don't need anyone else to do my work for me. How about I do this and you do something else?"

"Something else such as?" Dyphestive asked as he wrapped his fingers around stalks of corn and tossed them out.

"Look under the wagon," she said.

"You look under the wagon."

Grey Cloak stepped in. "If you'd like, I'll look under the wagon. I don't think I've ever looked under a wagon before."

"No!" Dyphestive and Beak said simultaneously.

Grey Cloak backed off. He noticed Beak's resemblance to Adanadel. She was attractive, with strong, refined features, but her crooked nose was puzzling. "It sounds to me like the two of you have some unresolved issues."

As Beak slung stalks of corn aside, she gave him a heated stare. "Stay put, elf."

"My name's Grey Cloak." He offered his hand. "Beak, is it?"

"Don't make me plant this cornstalk in you. Now get out of the way," she warned.

Grey Cloak lifted his palms and stepped back. "Testy. Sorry, I should have seen the signs of two young lovers quarreling."

Dyphestive gave him an embarrassed and dumbfounded look and said with incredulity, "What?"

Beak let out a dry laugh. "In his dreams."

She and Dyphestive started to quickly empty the wagon. Dyphestive gave him a subtle shrug. His blood brother could do nothing more. They would discover the shield in moments.

Somebody's about to have a really bad day.

He scanned his surroundings. The courtyards were clear of any guests, leaving only the Honor Guards, Monarch Knights, servants, and Monarchs on the grounds. The Monarchs stood in their lavish clothing, watching from the castle's tiers and windows, talking with one another and overlooking the grounds. The Monarch Knights gave the orders, and the Honor Guards executed the searches.

Grey Cloak searched for any avenue of escape. He didn't see one. *There has to be a way.*

A flock of yonders whizzed overhead. They spread over the courtyards, flying across the grounds. From one of the castle entrances came a group of men and women in purple-and-gold-checkered robes, escorted by a pair of Monarch Knights.

"Great, the enchanters are here," Sergeant Tinison said with disgust.

Dyphestive and Beak stopped to look.

Grey Cloak's blood froze. *From bad to worse.*

He caught Dyphestive's eye and fluttered his hands like a bird, then made a drinking motion by tipping his thumb to his lips like a jug. Dyphestive shook his head.

Eyeing the yonder scouring the area above, Grey Cloak said, "Sometimes I wish I could fly."

Beak scowled at him. "Stitch your lips." She resumed clearing out the wagon.

Grey Cloak gave Dyphestive a heated stare. "Don't you wish you could fly, Dyphestive?"

Dyphestive gave him a blank look.

"Wait, you two know each other?" Beak asked.

"Well, I thought so. We started on the same day," Grey Cloak said. "Captain Cleotus recruited us."

"Really?" She kept hauling cornstalks out of the wagon and eyeing him. "My father was great friends with him."

The wagon was almost empty. Grey Cloak could see his cloak showing underneath the cornstalks. "Can I head back now?"

Dyphestive's eyes grew the moment he saw the cloak. He started tossing cornstalks back in the wagon.

"What are you doing, buffoon?" Beak asked him.

"Loading the wagon," he admitted sheepishly. "I thought we were finished."

"I don't know about you, but the job isn't done until it's thoroughly done." Beak grabbed a handful of cornstalks and slung them out of the wagon. Her gaze caught the cloak. "What's this?"

Grey Cloak eased his hand into his pocket. "Oh, there it is. That's my cloak. I must have absentmindedly buried it. Thank you so very much for helping me find it. I would have hated to lose it."

Beak peeled the cloak back with her fingers. Her eyes widened. She jerked the cloak all the way back and gasped.

Codd's shield shone against the sun. She lifted her eyes to Grey Cloak's and caught his guilty look.

"It's not what you think," he said.

She drew her sword. "Thief!"

24

Grey Cloak eased a flashing out of his pocket and raised his hands. Honor Guards came rushing over along with the yonders hovering above. "If you'll give me a moment, I can explain everything," he said.

"Seize him!" Sergeant Tinison hollered.

Dyphestive slipped behind Grey Cloak and pulled his hands behind his back. As he did so, he whispered in his blood brother's ear, "Should I close my eyes now?"

With yonders circling overhead, Grey Cloak replied, "Yes." He dropped the flashing.

Boooomph!

As Dyphestive's hands loosened, Grey Cloak jumped into the wagon, donned his cloak, and grabbed the shield. No one was looking his direction, and everyone was shielding their eyes. The yonders dropped from the sky like dead birds, and he jumped out of the wagon holding the massive shield overhead. He could only see one way out: up and over the castle wall.

This is madness.

At full speed, Grey Cloak ran toward the portcullis and headed up the stone staircase on the backside. Many of the soldiers on the wall had been caught looking toward the flashing and were still rubbing their eyes. He plowed them over.

At the top of the wall, he was confronted by two men in plate-mail armor and helms. They were Monarch Knights, the castle's elite. The formidable men drew their longswords and advanced as one.

Grey Cloak lowered the shield and charged them at full speed. "Yaaaaaaah!" Codd's shield slammed into the knights' longswords as they struck. A resounding *kraaaaang* followed. The shield absorbed the blows and knocked the knights backward. Grey Cloak plowed right over them.

Behind the battements, Grey Cloak stopped and took a quick look over the side. It was a straight thirty-foot fall into the moat and another thirty-plus feet across. The behemoth-sized moat monsters lurked just below the waters, waiting to strike.

Can I jump it? Can I swim it fast enough? Zooks, what have I gotten myself into?

All of a sudden, the shield swung him around with a life of its own. A ballista bolt fired from one of the high towers would have skewered his back. Instead, the over-sized shaft of deadly metal ricocheted off the shield. Another bolt streaked through the sky with pinpoint precision. Grey Cloak watched it bounce off the shield like a dart falling from a board.

He eyed the shield.

This thing is fantastic.

The soldiers' eyes had cleared, and they advanced from both sides of the walls. Over two dozen Honor Guards and Monarch Knights closed in, escorted by giant winged eyeballs.

Grey Cloak crept between the castle's battlements and hid behind the shield. Ballista bolts whistled overhead and blasted off the shield, chipping rocks from the battlements.

A trio of yonders dropped in behind him, hovering in the air, keeping their distance.

"Oh, go away, ugly things!" he shouted.

The moat monsters gathered in the murky waters below.

He could hear the soldiers' heavy footsteps closing in.

Grey Cloak stuck his tongue out at the yonders and jumped. With his free hand, he grabbed one of the yonders by the wings and dragged it down with him. The gray folds of the Cloak of Legends billowed out. Grey Cloak floated down slowly to the astonishment of the soldiers leaning over the wall and shouting in dismay. Ballista bolts rocketed by.

Grey Cloak's feet dangled only twenty feet above the surging moat monsters, whose massive jaws snapped in anticipation. Aided by his cloak's magic, he sank to his doom. In a few moments, the moat monsters would chew him to bits.

"Well, if I'm going to die," he said to the eyeball that he cradled to his chest, "I'm not going to die alone. You're going first."

The yonder quivered like a frightened puppy.

"And just so you know, I only took the shield to save a friend. I plan to return it." With his fist locked around its wings, he hurled the yonder into the mouth of the largest moat monster, which swallowed it whole. "Ick."

No more ballista bolts whistled by him. He lowered the shield and looked at the crowd waiting for him to die. He strapped the shield across his arm, saluted them all, and said, "For Zora."

The moat monsters jumped from the waters, nipping at his toes. He lifted his knees to his chest. "I'm all out of tricks. Or am I?"

He fumbled to find the Figurine of Heroes in his pocket. It was his last hope. He started to say the words, but he caught something hurtling at him out of the corner of his eye. Dyphestive slammed into him while at the same time scooping Grey Cloak into his arms.

"Dyphestive, you're flying!"

"Forgive me for being so thick-skulled." Dyphestive flew

straight toward the city and away from the castle. "You know me. Sometimes it takes a while for things to sink in."

"Your timing couldn't be better," Grey Cloak said as he waved goodbye to the red-faced soldiers shaking their fists from Monarch Castle. "But I think your new friends might be disappointed."

"Where to now?" Dyphestive asked, the wind rustling his hair.

Grey Cloak pointed behind them. At least a dozen yonders were in pursuit. "As far away from them as possible."

25

Dyphestive blasted by the pigeons roosting in the eaves of the cathedrals, scattering them like leaves.

Grey Cloak laughed. "I hate pigeons."

"I thought you hated flying."

"I do, but not when my life depends on it." He glanced down at the people pointing up at them from the streets. Women in bonnets screamed and hauled their astonished children into stores. "What's the matter with them? They have to have seen men fly before."

"Where should I go?" Dyphestive asked.

"I don't know. Keep flying in a circle. I'm thinking."

The yonders stayed on them without getting too close, like some sort of aerial escort.

Grey Cloak patted his pockets. He was all out of flashings. "You know, I was surprised that you came for me. I thought you were mad."

"I thought you were mad."

"I was mad."

"I was too," Dyphestive said as he swooped over the rooftops. "But I couldn't sleep, and you know me. I sleep like a baby. I couldn't let you down, Grey. You're my best friend. I'll never let you down."

Grey Cloak nodded. "Not even over a woman. Beak was fetching, well, aside from her nose. In a strange sort of way, it was charming."

"She's too much like Adanadel, but I feel guilty. You know he died because of us."

"He died because he was a good man, and that's what good men do. He wouldn't want us to feel guilty." He watched the buildings pass by beneath him. "Head toward the Outer Ring, away from the bridges. There won't be so many soldiers there."

Dyphestive grinned.

Grey Cloak caught his smile. "What are you thinking?"

"You did it. You actually stole Codd's shield."

Grey Cloak smirked. "I did, didn't I? Did you ever doubt me?"

"I wouldn't put anything past you, especially when you put your mind to it, but I'd be a liar if I said I thought you could pull it off." Dyphestive flew over acres of farmland surrounding Monarch City. "That was amazing."

"Thank you, but stealing it is one thing. Getting away with it is another. Every soldier and giant eyeball in the city will be looking for us." A yonder flew within striking distance. He lashed out at it, but it drifted away. "I'm sorry you couldn't stay with the Honor Guard, but if we get caught, you might stay with them the rest of your life as they guard your dungeon cell."

"With you around, I probably won't be that lucky." Dyphestive suddenly dipped in the air. "Uh, do you have any idea how long that potion will last?"

"No idea. Why?"

Dyphestive shrugged as they skimmed the ground, heading toward the Outer Ring. "Because I think it's coming to an end." Dyphestive crashed on top of Grey Cloak. They slid through a vegetable garden, riding the shield like a sled, and plowed over a scarecrow that looked like an orc as they entered a cornfield.

Grey Cloak squeezed out from under Dyphestive's body. "Zooks, you're heavy. More corn." He flung an ear at a yonder and knocked it out of the sky. "Bull's-eye."

The blood brothers hurled one ear of corn after the other at the flying eyeball vermin, but the enchanted creatures scattered like flies.

Nothing but wide-open countryside, cottages, and farm buildings stood between them and the Outer Ring Moat of the city. "Soldiers will be galloping our way soon enough." He slapped Dyphestive on the shoulder. "Come on."

They ran toward the Outer Ring and stopped on the ledge. Grey Cloak walked along the lip, staring downward.

"You don't want to climb down there, do you?" Dyphestive asked.

"If we have to, but that isn't what I had in mind." He pointed down. "There!" Several dozen yards ahead, he could see water draining from the side of the cliff. "Those are huge drainage tunnels coming from the city. I saw them on the way in. We should fit." He ran until he stood over one then strapped the shield on Dyphestive's back and lowered himself over the edge. "Are you coming?"

"You know I'm not a strong climber." Dyphestive wiggled his beefy fingers. "They have trouble grabbing some things."

"We don't have a choice. We have to try. And it's only a few dozen feet down." He began to lower himself. Glancing at the yonders hovering around, he added, "Get moving!"

Dyphestive lowered himself over the rim. He looked like a giant terrapin with the shield on his back. His fingers found solid purchase on the first several feet of descent.

"Good, good," Grey Cloak said. "Take your time. Not a lot of time, but well, you know..."

Dyphestive looked down. "I think I have it." He slipped and crashed straight down into Grey Cloak, knocking them both off the cliff face.

"Noooo!" Grey Cloak cried as they fell. Dyphestive latched onto him like a tick. The Cloak of Legends feathered out, and they floated downward. "Stop squirming!" He stretched for the rock, trying to grab the rim of the drainage tunnel as they passed. He gripped the edge, but he couldn't hold on. Though the cloak had slowed them, their weight was still the same. Dyphestive was dragging him down, and Grey Cloak's fingers were slipping. "You're too heavy!"

Dyphestive swung his arm over Grey Cloak's head and fastened his fingers on the tunnel's lip. "I can hold on. Go!"

Grey Cloak climbed inside the six-foot-high pipe. He reached down and grabbed his brother's arm. "Get in here!"

"I have it." Dyphestive crawled on his elbows through the sloppy, stinky, trickling water and into the dark hole. He looked down the pipe. "What now? It stinks."

"It's either this way or down." Grey Cloak led the way.

They made it forty feet in the pipe and ran into a grid of corroded steel that blocked their passage. Grey Cloak locked his fingers around the bars and knocked his forehead against the steel. "And I wanted to be an adventurer."

Dyphestive tapped his shoulder. He had to stoop down to avoid hitting his head. "We still have company."

The yonders had followed them into the tunnel. The white globular eyeballs cast a green hue around them.

Grey Cloak sighed. "Thanks for the light, rodents." He pulled a dagger from one of his pockets and chased them out of the tunnel. "Haven't you seen enough?" He beat his chest. "Come and get me now, why don't you?"

"Grey?"

He turned. He could see Dyphestive's white grin. "What?"

"I can handle this," Dyphestive replied. He grabbed the metal grid at its base with his bare fingers. His shoulders bunched and heaved as he pulled backward.

The metal groaned and separated from the stone wall. Thrusting with his mighty legs and pulling with all his might, the red-faced young warrior peeled the metal back like a banana. He let out a deep breath and stepped aside. "After you."

Grey Cloak slipped through the gap. "You're the best brother an elf could ever have."

"Thanks." Dyphestive followed him and caught Grey Cloak's disapproving eye. "What?"

"We can't have them following us."

"Oh." Dyphestive turned around and pulled the metal back into place as a wall of glowing eyeballs watched.

Grey Cloak took one last moment to face them. He put his thumbs to his temples, wiggled his fingers, and let out a funny *phylllt* sound. He pushed his brother along, and they vanished into the dark sewer tunnel.

26

Night had fallen over Monarch City. It was day three of Zora's abduction, and every soldier in Monarch City combed the streets, looking for Grey Cloak and Dyphestive.

After hiding in the sewer pipes the majority of the day, the blood brothers finally caught a break, hit the cobblestone streets, and in the dark of night, stole back to Crane's apartment, where a group of soldiers were departing. Jakoby, Leena, and Than were waiting for them there.

Grey Cloak sat on the sofa, petting Streak, who was lying on his lap. Dyphestive sat beside him, drinking a jug of water. Leena had squeezed in between them.

Jakoby stood by the small kitchen stove, holding Codd's shield. "I can't believe I'm holding it. It's even bigger up close." He polished the front with the palm of his hand and hugged it. "I don't think any man has laid a finger on it in centuries." He eyed the brothers. "You've earned my respect. Great respect, and that does not come lightly. Saving me was one thing, but this, well, this is astonishing. Hah."

"So you weren't able to locate Zora?" Grey Cloak asked.

Than stood by the small bay window with his shoulder leaning against the wall and his arms crossed. His eyes combed the streets. "We took a chance and tried the dungeons that you freed us from again. They were waiting."

"You went back?" Grey Cloak asked.

"It seemed logical that they might hide her there and hope we would attempt a rescue. We sprang the trap and eliminated the dungeon as a possibility. We exposed the enemy's resources too," Than calmly said.

Grey Cloak ground his teeth. Whatever they did would have agitated Irsk Mondo. If anything, the rogue leader would have buried Zora deeper if not quicker. "What happened?"

"We came across one of Irsk's minions, Finton Slay, and the Iron Devils. It turns out that the Devils aren't ordinary thieves and assassins but ghouls that almost killed us. Thanks to Than, we live," Jakoby said.

"Thanks to Than, all of you almost died," Grey Cloak said dryly.

"It wasn't all his idea," Jakoby admitted.

The door handle to the apartment rattled. Jakoby stole over to the door, pulled his dagger, and hid to the side. Everyone quieted. The door quietly swung open, and a paunchy man with wavy hair entered. Jakoby slipped in behind him and brought him to the floor.

"Crane!" Dyphestive said.

"He's one of us," Grey Cloak added.

"Sorry about that," Jakoby said politely as he effortlessly hauled Crane back to his feet.

"I had a key," Crane replied with a bewildered look. "And it's my apartment."

Jakoby closed the door. "Jumpy times."

"I can see that." Crane unrolled a piece of parchment and handed it to Grey Cloak. "Literally."

Grey Cloak looked at a perfect picture of his and Dyphestive's faces. It read:

Wanted: Dead or Alive. Reward. 1000 gold chips each.

"That's a fortune!" Grey Cloak exclaimed. "Every man, woman, and child will be hunting us down."

"Well." Crane shrugged. "Not the rich ones. I just returned. What did you do?"

Grey Cloak pointed to the kitchen, where the shield leaned. "Stole Codd's shield."

Crane's mouth dropped into an *o*. He half-covered his mouth. "Why did you do that? *How* did you do that?"

"We crossed the Dark Addler. They kidnapped Zora

and wanted the shield in exchange for her," Grey Cloak said.

Crane sniffed. "What stinks?"

"We escaped through the sewers."

"I see. Stink happens." Crane sauntered over to the blackwood wine cabinet. Using a small key, he opened the doors and removed a glass bottle with a round bottom. "It's called Brandy. She's a fine gal. Any partakers? I hate to drink alone."

"Knights don't drink," Jakoby said as he came forward, "but I'm not a knight anymore. Fill one up for me."

Crane filled up two pewter goblets and corked the bottle. "Now what?"

"With everyone in the city combing the streets for us, I can't even get to Irsk Mondo." Grey Cloak picked Streak up off his lap and set him on the table.

Crane sipped his brandy. "Who's your contact?"

"Orpah the orc. She'll be waiting at the Tavern Dwellers Inn. She's probably the one who drew those pictures," he said. "That place will be filled with people looking for us. They know we used to work there."

"All of us are wanted," Than added.

"Sounds like I'm in good company." Crane polished off his brandy. "Wait here. I'll set up a meeting." He refilled his goblet. "One for the road. Tell me, this Orpah, any distinguishing marks?" He shrugged his eyebrows. "Is she pretty?"

"Don't worry," Grey Cloak said as he showed Crane the door. "You can't miss her."

"Perfect," Crane said. "Sounds like the kind of woman I'm looking for."

27

Crane returned with a guilty expression. "Sorry, but there was nothing I could do. Orpah's a tough negotiator. Cute but tough."

Grey Cloak's jaw tightened. Once again, Irsk Mondo was calling the shots, and once again, he had to cave to the fiendish goblin-elf's demands. "Didn't you explain that the entire city is looking for us?"

"Orpah said that's the reason for the additional discretion. It's Irsk's place or no place at all," Crane said.

Grey Cloak picked Streak up by the tail and let the dragon latch onto his back. He winced. "I don't guess those claws are going to get any softer." He swung his cloak over his shoulders. "And he insists that only I come?"

"Those are the terms."

"You can't do this alone. You know you can't trust him," Dyphestive said. "I'm coming too."

"I'll take my chances," Grey Cloak said.

"If you go, Dyphestive, they'll scatter like rats, and we'll never see Zora again," Crane warned. "Orpah promised me that. Again, I'm sorry."

Grey Cloak laid a hand on his brother's shoulder. "Don't worry. I'll figure something out. I always do."

"At least we know where you're going," Jakoby said as he opened the apartment door. "We'll be close by but not too close."

Grey Cloak nodded, lifted Codd's shield, which he'd wrapped in burlap, and eyed Crane. "Lead the way."

Crane headed down the stairs. "Orpah gave specific instructions and said she'd make sure the way was clear. I'll take you as far as the sun gods' cathedral. I'll stay close." He peered out into the street and led them through the dank back alleys and stopped for a peek around the corner. Across the road, a candle with a blue flame burned in a window. "There."

Grey Cloak and Crane jetted across the street into a general store's open front door. A man with long sleeves and a vest met them there. Hair hung over his eyes. He carried the blue candle. They followed him to the back of the store and crossed through an entrance that connected one store to another. They went down a set of steps into a musty stone corridor that ran beneath the road.

Whoa! No wonder I couldn't figure out where we were going before. It's an entire subterranean network.

A network of tunnels ran underneath the city, separate from the sewer lines that the soldiers had already been searching. The tunnels connected city block to city block and opened into the basements of many stores. They popped up inside a candle, tobacco, and incense shop on the same block as the cathedral.

The long-haired rogue said in a rusty voice, "Come on."

Grey Cloak gave Crane one last look.

"I'll wait right here," the older man assured him.

Grey Cloak and the rogue jetted into a side entrance underneath the cathedral's grand stair. Another rogue, a lean lizardman with a droopy head, opened the door for him. He was met by a host of Iron Devils, twelve in all. Each held a sword with hands wrapped in old cloth.

Ghouls. Sickening.

The Devils led him straight through the cathedral's basement, which was a network of ancient crypts of high-ranking priests, ornately decorated with stone sculptures of the sun gods, and sarcophagi plated in precious metals. They entered a stairwell and moved silently upward into a tunnel that backtracked to the cathedral's main foyer. One of the Devils pointed toward the apse. The pews in the nave ran nearly a hundred rows deep.

Grey Cloak entered, and the brass double doors closed behind him. The pews were modestly filled with people wearing iron masks and crimson robes. They turned their metal eye slits toward him.

What's going on? Is this my wedding day?

At the end of the aisles, sitting in the high priest's chair, was Irsk Mondo. The half goblin, half elf leaned back in his throne with a foot up on the chair and his arm dangling over the side. He still wore Zora's Scarf of Shadows around his neck. To his right was Finton Slay, the bald necromancer, dressed in all black. Kneeling between them was a disheveled Zora with a gag in her mouth.

Grey Cloak locked eyes with Zora and fast-walked down the long aisle, carrying the shield in both hands.

"That's close enough," Irsk said in his condescending tone, stopping Grey Cloak twenty feet from his grand chair. He leaned forward, eyeing the shield that was covered by a blanket. "You've created quite a stir. Quite a stir." He tapped his fingertips together. "Why, the Monarchs hold the Dark Addler responsible. Can you believe such a thing?" He combed his greasy hair behind his long ears. "Let me see it."

Grey Cloak dropped the blanket on the ground, fully revealing the shield in all its glory. "The shield is delivered, as you requested. Now release my friend."

Irsk showed off a mouthful of long, crooked teeth. "Not so fast. I have to test its authenticity."

"What sort of game are you playing, Irsk? My picture is everywhere. The entire city is tearing down the walls trying to find me. You know it's real. Stop fooling," Grey Cloak said. "Let Zora go!"

Irsk's hollow laughter echoed throughout the cathedral's chambers. "I've been doing this a long time. A very long time. Codd's armor is often replicated." He reached down and picked up a flail with a spiked metal ball attached to the end. He stood, stretching toward the rafters, over seven feet in height, with the crude weapon hanging by his side and walked down the steps.

"This is Bone Crusher. A personal weapon of mine." Irsk started to gently swing it. The spikes glowed. "A single strike can bust apart shields of the finest craft. Now we shall see whether this shield is real or a replica."

Grey Cloak braced himself behind the shield.

Irsk wound the flail up, creating a ring of energy with an angry golden glow. It sounded like a swarm of buzzing hornets. With a snap of his wrist, he struck the nearest pew. The ancient stone exploded, and a hunk of rock went flying toward an Iron Devil in the back.

With triumph in his dark eyes, Irsk wound the weapon up again. Using both hands, he swung the flail into the shield with all his might.

Grey Cloak waited to be knocked from his feet. Instead, Codd's shield hummed like a low-keyed tuning fork. He stole a glance at Irsk.

The leader of the Dark Addler grimaced and flicked his hands, one after the other, as if shaking away pain. Irsk pitched the flail aside. "It's authentic."

Finton Slay nodded.

"You have your shield. Now let Zora ago," Grey Cloak demanded. "And when I say go, I mean both of us walk out of here alive."

Irsk stroked the scraggly hairs on his chin. "You do realize that you're safer inside than outside. I can offer my protection."

Grey Cloak scoffed. "I want nothing to do with vermin like you."

"Oh, don't be so quick to judge. A man of your skill, and so young, would do well in the service of a man like me. I have to admit, you impressed me."

"I don't want any part of the Dark Addler."

"Don't be so hasty, because you might not have a choice." Irsk resumed his seat on the chair. "Think about it. You're a wanted man. The Monarchs won't stop until they have you. You need protection. All of you need protection. Besides, you owe me."

"Owe you for what? I brought the shield."

"There's the matter of the other prisoners your friends freed."

"The shield is worth one hundred times anything you might have lost. Quit playing games with me, and let Zora go." He eased forward. "I thought there was honor among thieves."

Irsk spread his hands. "I have to admit that I'm not very used to this. Typically, when I give men impossible tasks, they fall flat on their faces, but not in your case. No, you actually pulled it off. It makes me curious."

"I'm a determined elf. You underestimated me."

"I don't like being made a fool of. I have a reputation to protect," Irsk said.

"But you have the shield. What more could you ask for?"

Irsk tapped his fingernails on the arm of his chair and shifted back and forth in his seat. "This is very difficult because I like you. You carry yourself with the edge that I need. Let me offer one last time. Join the Dark Addler. You'll need my protection."

"No," Grey Cloak said firmly. "Let Zora go."

"The Monarchs will hunt you down and flay you alive," Irsk warned.

"I'll take my chances."

Irsk leaned back in his chair. "Speaking of chances, I can't take any and have you lead the Monarchs back to me. It seems that you leave me with little choice. Finton Slay?"

"Yes, Dark Addler," the hollow-eyed necromancer said in his cryptic voice.

"Slay them."

Surprise, surprise.

Grey Cloak's fingers fished coins from his pockets as he watched the Iron Devils rise from their seats. He summoned his wizardry and charged the coins with power. He gave Irsk Mondo a warning glance. "Are you sure you don't want to reconsider?"

"I stand by my decision."

As the Devils advanced, Grey Cloak said, "So be it. Zora, duck!"

Zora flattened on the floor as Grey Cloak hurled a handful of glowing coins at Irsk and Finton.

With catlike speed, Irsk dove out of his chair. Several coins hit the chair and blew the wood to pieces. The rest of the coins hit Finton Slay square in the chest and blasted the flat-footed wizard backward behind the altar.

Irsk pushed himself off the floor, snatched up his flail, and shouted with rage, "Kill them! Kill them! Kill them!"

Grey Cloak had counted at least fifty of the Iron Devils in the pews on his way in. It appeared that even more were popping up. Some moved with a jerkiness while others were more fluid, like normal men. He swung his shield around and knocked two close attackers over and hollered, "Zora, come on!"

Zora rolled away from Irsk just as he brought the flail down to smash her head open. She popped up and sped toward Grey Cloak. By the time she arrived, she'd wriggled out of her bindings and removed her gag. "Do you call this a rescue?"

"I missed you too." He plowed into two more sword-bearing attackers filling the aisle.

"Is that why you took so long?" She ducked under a sword swipe and kicked her attacker in the groin.

"Well, you were pretty steamed that last time we spoke. I thought you needed more time." Grey Cloak jumped from one pew to the next with Zora right behind him.

The masked Devils came at them from all directions, slicing and chopping at their knees, ankles, and toes. All of the exits were blocked by crimson-cloaked bodies, and every door was barred shut, sealing the desperate heroes in. There was nowhere to turn. Nowhere to run.

Irsk Mondo jumped the pews two at a time and closed the gap. He pinned Grey Cloak and Zora between two columns. "You fools can't last forever, shield or no shield."

Using Bone Crusher, he whacked the shield with one hard, resounding blow after another.

Several of the Iron Devils climbed the columns like spiders and prepared to jump down on top of them with blades poised to kill.

Grey Cloak and Zora hunkered down underneath the shield. She kissed his cheek.

"What was that for?"

She gripped him tightly by the waist. "I wanted to thank you for trying."

Irsk pounded away. The Devils jumped.

"You can thank me later. I'm not finished yet," Grey Cloak said through clenched teeth. He snagged the Figurine of Heroes out of his pocket and started saying the enchanted words under his breath. The strange syllables twisted inside his mouth as he spewed them. He rolled the figurine under the shield to the pew rows below Irsk's legs.

"What's this trick?" Irsk demanded as he backed away from the shield.

An inky black smoke spilled over the floor and spread rapidly.

"We're going to die, aren't we?" Zora covered her nose. "Tatiana warned you about abusing that."

"We were about to die, one way or the other," he said.

"Who are you?" Irsk stammered.

The tip of a scaly black tail swiped underneath Codd's

shield. A cold and husky-voiced woman answered, "I am Selene."

Streak popped his head out from under Grey Cloak's cloak. His pink tongue flickered out of his mouth.

Zora let out a squeal and clutched her chest. "You could have told me you had him packed in there."

"In all the excitement, I forgot. He's like a part of my body."

Streak scrambled down to the floor and squeezed underneath the shield.

"Get back here!"

"Whoever you are, you won't last long," Irsk Mondo warned. The flail, Bone Breaker, hummed by his side. "Iron Devils, kill her!"

"Her?" Grey Cloak and Zora shared a surprised look. They peeked over the rim of the shield.

A beautiful woman stood in the smoke, surrounded by Irsk's minions. Her long raven-colored hair had a white streak on one side. Her sublime body was covered in black scales, like a dragon, and a long tail flicked from side to side beside her. She had a dangerous look in her violet eyes, and she held a dagger burning with purple flame.

"Whoa," Grey Cloak said.

The dragon woman stared down at Irsk. "Whoever you are, I don't like you." She glanced at the Iron Devils like they were fleas. "You will all die today."

Irsk spun his flail in a bright blur between them. "We'll see about that, dragon wench! Slay her!"

The Devils converged on Selene as one. Irsk struck out with them.

In a blur of dazzling speed, Selene pumped her dagger into attacker after attacker. Their bodies burned from the inside out, catching their robes on fire. Her black tail cracked like a whip, and four of the Devils went flying head over heels. A bolt of fire blasted out of her hand, knocking one ghoul back into another.

Irsk Mondo saw a clean shot and brought the flail down on her head. She slipped under the attack in the blink of an eye and punched him hard in the chest, sending Irsk flying into a column. His back cracked against the stone, and the flail went flying from his fingers.

Streak jumped on a ghoul's face and coiled his tail around the man's neck. Grey Cloak handed Zora a dagger from his pocket and grabbed his sword. They sprang into action.

"Careful, they're ghouls," Grey Cloak said.

"Some are, some aren't. You can take the ones that are," Zora said as she jumped behind a man and stabbed him in the back.

Selene tore through the ranks of the dead and living like a saw blade in a windmill. The crimson assassins' blades shattered against her steely hide. She made them pay for it with dagger thrusts in the chest that exploded them from the inside. The dead fell. The living died in droves. Yet more came.

Grey Cloak flicked a handful of magic-fired coins, sending more men flying over the pews.

"Where'd you pick that up?" Zora exclaimed as she ducked a razor-sharp thrust and kicked a man's iron mask off his face.

"Gunder Island. I'll explain later."

Selene tore through the ranks of Iron Devils with ease. One ghoul exploded after another. From out of nowhere, a blast of hellish fire knocked her from her feet and sent her crashing through the backrests of the stone pews. She lay still in dusty gray debris, the colorful moonlight through the stained glass windows shining on her body.

Finton Slay stood on the stage, his hands smoking with radiant power. A victorious sneer stretched across his face as Irsk Mondo limped over.

"Well done." Irsk patted his top henchman on the back. "Well done indeed."

Selene rose from the smoke with fire in her eyes.

Finton's haunting eyes grew to the size of saucers. "Impossible, I hit her with everything I had!"

The dark-haired warrior advanced. "Then you're a dead man."

"Stop her!" Irsk commanded. "Stop her!"

The Iron Devils swarmed her in droves of ten and twenty. They piled on her arms and legs.

Grey Cloak and Zora fought with everything they had, but the numbers were too many. "Zora, stay close!"

The half elf had a weary look in her eyes. Her dagger hung at her side. "I don't have anything left. There are too many."

Selene killed the men two at a time. She was a juggernaut of power, but even she was overwhelmed.

"Streak, give us some cover," Grey Cloak commanded.

Smoke rose from the floor, obscuring the enemies' vision.

Grey Cloak shoved Zora to the floor. "Stay down for now." He sprang up behind two men and cut them down with a single swipe of his blade. One dropped dead. The other turned. It was a ghoul with glinting eyes behind its metal mask. Grey Cloak lopped its head off with a quick stroke of steel.

The Devils swarmed. He couldn't kill them all but tried, thrust after thrust, until a ghoul grabbed ahold of him. "Eeeargh!"

As Grey Cloak fought to stay alive and on his feet, he glimpsed movement on the other side of the surrounding violet-and-crimson stained glass windows above. In a violent explosion, the colorful shards of glass burst into the cathedral.

Four figures descended from separate windows and landed on their feet in the pews. Dyphestive, Than, Jakoby, and Leena arrived with fight in their eyes.

With Lythlenion's war mace in hand, Dyphestive shouted at the top of his lungs, "It's thunder time!"

Two of the Iron Devils converged on him with stunning speed. He cranked the war mace back and sent them flying.

Leena's nunchakus spun with fire. She knocked an iron mask off a man's face and clobbered him with lightning-quick strikes.

Blood surged through Grey Cloak's veins, and he shook off his attackers and punched holes in their bellies.

Jakoby let out his battle cry, "Long live the monarchy!"

Than furiously pulled crimson-robed men away from Selene and slung them over the pews. His wild hair flew all around him. His brown eyes burned with golden light.

The Devils lost the upper hand but fought on. Leena busted their bones with rapid strikes, cracking jaws and elbows. Dyphestive fought a ghoul on his back while he pounded another one to the ground. Jakoby batted swords aside and skewered men with his own. Everyone fought for their lives in a clamor of pain and battle cries. The cathedral of the sun gods turned into a bloody battlefield.

Grey Cloak chopped a Devil lizardman down. Out of the corner of his eye, he caught Irsk and Finton backing farther into the apse. Standing on a pile of the dead, he pointed his sword at them. "Don't let them get away!"

Dozens of the Iron Devils fell under the heroes' might, but still more came.

"Retreat!" Irsk ordered. He winked at Grey Cloak and grabbed Finton's shoulder. In a puff of smoke, they vanished.

The surviving Devils scurried out through the doors like drowning rats.

Than lifted a man over his shoulders, revealing the struggling dragon woman underneath. His golden eyes widened. "Selene!" He flung the man into a pillar and embraced her. "You're here, how?"

"I don't know," she said as her tail lashed out. She knocked a mask from an attacker's face and sent him spinning over the pews. "Where are we?"

"Gapoli. Another world. How did you get here?" Than asked again.

"I don't know."

He wrapped his arms around her. "I missed you. You look beautiful."

"And you look old." Selene broke their embrace. Her sublime body started to fade into smoke. "What's happening?"

Than's fingers passed through her. "Noooo! Noooo!"

"Keep fighting, Dragon. We'll find you!" Selene stated as she vanished.

"I love you!" he shouted.

Selene was gone.

Grey Cloak approached Than. "You knew her?"

Than had fire in his eyes. He grabbed Grey Cloak by the collar and lifted him off his feet. "She's my wife. Bring her back. Bring her back!"

"I don't have any control over who comes and who goes," he said.

Than shook him. "How did you do that?"

"You know, you're a lot stronger than you appear. Will you please put me down?"

Than lowered him to the ground with a hopeless look in his eyes. "Sorry." Than sat down on a pew and sighed.

Zora drew near Grey Cloak with the Figurine of Heroes in her hands.

He put his arm around her. "I'm glad you're all right."

With weary eyes she said, "I am, but I'm exhausted."

Grey Cloak sat down by Than as the others gathered around. All of them were scratched up and splattered with living and undead blood.

Grey Cloak fished the potion of restoration out of his pocket and handed it to Zora. "Pass it around." He showed Than the figurine. "I have no control over who or what it summons. All I know is that they come from other worlds."

"May I?" Than asked.

Grey Cloak held it to his chest. "No, it's mine."

Than frowned and said dejectedly, "At least we both know the other is alive."

"Did you say that she's your wife?"

Than nodded.

"I'm glad she was on our side. She came across as frosty." Grey Cloak patted Than on the back. "Everyone, the old hermit has a wife. How about that?"

Leena drank some of the potion and made a bitter face. She handed it to Jakoby. He passed it to Zora, whose arm was bloody. She drank the rest of it.

Dyphestive slapped Than on the back. "Congratulations. I only caught a glimpse of her, but she was very pretty. How long have you been married?"

"A thousand years or so," Than said.

"Oh." Dyphestive exchanged doubtful looks with the others.

Grey Cloak rose and looked about. "Codd's shield!"

The shield lay between two columns. Dyphestive fetched it.

Grey Cloak let out a sigh of relief. He wiped the sweat from his brow. "Whew! We did it." He tucked the figurine away, felt eyes on him, and looked up. "Zooks."

Over a dozen yonders entered through the broken stained glass windows. The flying eyeballs slowly floated above them.

Grey Cloak gave them a casual wave. "I guess they found us." He stood with Streak in his arms. "Now let's hope I can explain all of this."

The heroes pushed through the double doors of the cathedral. Their jaws dropped as they froze. It looked like the entire Monarch army had filled the streets. Monarch Knights, Honor Guards, and horse-drawn wagons and chariots stretched on as far as the eye could see.

Grey Cloak set Streak down. "Hide, little brother, hide."

Dyphestive set the shield before their outnumbered group, and they raised their hands in surrender.

31

"Dungeons aren't so bad once you get used to them," Grey Cloak said. His arms and legs were shackled to the wall. "It's the additional restraints that make it so unpleasant. Well, that and the smell."

He wasn't alone in his shackles. Dyphestive, Zora, Than, Jakoby, and Leena were in the same condition, stripped down to their undergarments with their backsides against the wet, moldy wall. At least all of them shared the same large cell.

"At least we have one another's company," Dyphestive said with a warm grin.

Jakoby sighed. "It will probably be the guillotine or hanging. It wouldn't surprise me one bit if it wasn't tomorrow at first light. I knew my past would catch up with me. My only hope was to have a few more years to live."

"Why do the Monarchs want to kill you?" Grey Cloak asked.

"Some Monarchs are good, and some are bad. I crossed the bad ones, and it was their word against mine," the dark-skinned knight said. "The same thing happened to my brother, Adanadel. That's why we left the Monarch Knights. They were being corrupted. I caught them slave trading with the Dark Addler. They were trying to make me a slave as well."

Dyphestive leaned forward in his chains. Grey Cloak was on the end to his right. Leena was on his left, followed by Zora, Jakoby, and Than. "Jakoby, I met your niece, Beak—I mean Shannon. She's training to be an Honor Guard and strives to be a knight. I never thought to warn her about what you said. I-I," he stammered, shamefaced. "I didn't want to tell her that I knew her father since he died because of me."

"Don't blame yourself," Jakoby assured him. "Revealing that information might have placed you and her in greater danger. When the time comes, if it comes"—he eyed his glum surroundings—"you'll know when to tell her."

Grey Cloak watched water drip from the ceiling. They were secured behind a row of solid steel bars two dozen feet away. The steel door was locked with a padlock, which he knew he could pick easily, but he didn't have his cloak anymore. The soldiers had taken it.

He looked down the row of heroes. "So this is Talon."

"What?" Jakoby asked.

"That's the name we chose for ourselves. Rather, Adanadel and Dalsay did when they recruited us." He smiled. "Now that I think about it, we've had many members, albeit briefly. Zora is the oldest member left."

"I'm not the oldest," she disagreed.

"That's not what I meant," he assured her as he looked her way. "It started with Adanadel, Dalsay, Browning, Tanlin, Tatiana, and Zora. We added Rhonna, Lythlenion, and Bowbreaker."

"I miss Bowbreaker," Zora said sadly. "He's so—"

"Reginald the Razor and Grunt came along. Now, the three of you," Grey Cloak said, speaking to Jakoby, Leena, and Than. "We are adventurers. This is what adventurers do. Did I miss anyone?"

"Does Cotton count?" Dyphestive asked of the old halfling that he almost killed when he was a Doom Rider.

"Ah, I suppose."

"Is there an oath we must swear to become a member of Talon?" Jakoby asked.

"No, we mainly do it for treasure and dragon charms, which we give to the Wizard Watch. Somewhere along the way, we should save the world, but I think Tatiana is working on that now."

"I see," Jakoby said. "This group has had many people. Perhaps the others will rescue us."

"I doubt it, but we'll find a way." Grey Cloak noticed

Than's head hanging low over his chest, and Than hadn't said a word. "Is he well?"

Jakoby managed to kick Than.

Than lifted his head. "I am well, but my heart yearns to see my wife. You must tell me more about the Figurine of Heroes. Has it summoned others from my world?"

"I have no idea what world the others came from," Grey Cloak said.

Than stared at Grey Cloak with his hair hanging over his eyes. "Pry deeper into your gray matter, and pull out more details."

"Let's see. There was Selene, your wife, the dragon lady, an elf with a staff, very polite by the way," Grey Cloak added, "who called himself Bayzog?"

"Bayzog!" Than made and incredulous look. "I haven't seen him in hundreds of years. I thought he was dead. How is that possible?"

Grey Cloak shrugged. "Shall I continue? This seems to be helping. Uh, aside from Bayzog, there was a sorcerer who called himself Finster. Very cold and calculating. Merciless too. He turned my enemies' swords against them and turned them into meat on sticks." His chains rattled when he scratched his head. "Who else?"

"There was the muscle-bound warrior who rode a two-headed dog." Zora couldn't fight her big smile. "I wouldn't mind summoning him again."

Than's gold-flecked eyes widened. "Did he carry a

double-bladed war axe and have a gusty voice filled with thunder?"

Grey Cloak and Dyphestive glanced at one another.

Zora said, "Oh yes."

"Is he from your world too?" Dyphestive asked.

"No, he's from another," Than answered.

"How many worlds have you been to?" Grey Cloak asked.

"Many, but believe me when I say no world is fouler than Bish," Than said.

"Well, this one is looking pretty bad," Grey Cloak commented as he tugged on his chains. "Jakoby, can you give us some idea of what to expect? Or are they going to make us rot here in these chains?"

"It's difficult to know what to expect when it comes to the Monarchs," Jakoby answered. "The worst thing you can do is make them look bad. Believe me when I say that they're trying to cover up the damage to their reputation that you caused." He cracked his neck from side to side. "Once they assess the damage, I imagine that we will get a chance to face our accusers. And believe me, there will be plenty of witnesses to our crimes. But at least we'll be given a chance to speak. Matters like this are entertainment to them. They thrive on drama. The truth is, some Monarchs might even support our efforts, but it will only be for show."

"You make it all sound pointless," Dyphestive said.

"Look at us." Jakoby eyeballed everyone in the row. "All of us have committed crimes against them. I attacked them, and Leena did too. You," he said to Grey Cloak, "stole the shield, and Dyphestive aided you. I'm not really sure what Than did."

"Or Zora," Grey Cloak added. "But we were blackmailed."

"We'll all be appointed an advocate. If you can convince them of your innocence, perhaps they can convince others." Jakoby grimaced. "Otherwise, I imagine we will all die or be buried in the dungeons until our flesh rots from our bones."

32

____

"This wouldn't be so bad if we could sit down," Zora said. Her hair was messed up, and her legs quivered. "How long do they expect us to remain like this?"

"I don't know." Grey Cloak's guilt grew with every passing hour. It seemed that his friends were suffering because of him, all because he wanted to be an adventurer and have a fortune to himself. "Be strong, Zora." Then he hollered, "Guards! Guards! Some of us could use a reprieve!"

"Don't waste your breath on my account," Zora said indignantly. "I can yell for myself."

"I was only trying to help," he said, trying to catch her eye.

She wouldn't look at him. "Do I look like I need your help? Worry about yourself," Zora fired back.

"Sorry," he snapped.

"Save your apologies!"

Grey Cloak blanched.

Dyphestive's eyebrows lifted, and he wasn't the only one. Jakoby and Than looked surprised too. Leena, however, looked perfectly comfortable with her eyes closed.

Guilty butterflies fluttered inside Grey Cloak's stomach as he second-guessed himself. *I never should have rescued the Gunthys. That's how all of this started. I never would have imagined saving someone could have such dire consequences. Now look at where I am. All of my friends are in the dungeon, and I've lost everything.*

"Everyone, keep your chins up," Jakoby said. "The Monarchs might be quirky, but they aren't trying to torture us. That will come later, maybe."

Zora let out a long sigh. "Grey Cloak, I'm not mad at you so much as I am at myself," she admitted. "I tried to escape on my own, and I failed. And I'm really mad that the scarf Tanlin gave me is gone. That fiend, Irsk, still has it. Back in the cathedral, I should have grabbed it."

"Yes, you should have," Grey Cloak replied. "I mean, what were you doing anyway, fighting for your life and trying to save others? You are so selfish, Zora. You should be ashamed."

"If you're trying to make me laugh, it's not working."

Jakoby chuckled.

"And what are you laughing at, Jakoby?" Grey Cloak asked. "You were swinging your sword like a blind man fighting with a broom."

The former Monarch Knight erupted in laughter.

"Did you even kill anybody, or were you too busy tucking them in for the night?" He saw Zora chuckle. "And, Dyphestive, what sort of battle cry was that? How did it go? 'It's thunder time!' Who are you trying to frighten? Children?"

By that time, everyone was laughing out loud except for Leena, who still had her eyes squeezed closed.

"And look at the man we follow, a hermit named Thanadiliditis. Not only is he older than all of us put together plus a thousand years, but he looks every bit one thousand years too. Tell us, Than, what is your secret to longevity? Do you bathe in dragon's milk, or is it because you married centuries younger?"

Than gave him a heated look. Everyone fell silent.

"Actually," Than offered, "she's much older than I am."

The dungeon erupted in laughter so loud that the metal bars hummed like tuning forks. Everyone's faces grew as red as beets. Their chains rattled when they clutched at their guts.

Jakoby was the loudest one of all. "Bwah-haaaa-haaaa-haah!"

Zora let out a couple of snorts that she tried to cover with her hands, but she couldn't stop laughing.

A blinding flash of light interrupted their laughter. Someone with a booming voice said, "ENOUGH!"

33

The imprisoned members of Talon watched in silence as a man materialized inside their cell in a puff of smoke. He was above average in height and broad shouldered with white woolen hair that fit his head like a helmet parted in the middle. Fine rings covered his fingers. He wore lime-green silk robes decorated with black geometric symbols. He had a warm countenance but was odd looking with his hard eyes, and he appeared to be aggravated.

The newcomer fanned the smoke away with his robes and said in a deep voice, "I don't think I've ever heard laughter in the Monarchs' dungeons." His voice carried well. "Wooza! I suppose there's a first time for everything."

"Who are you?" Grey Cloak asked. "Are you here to save us?"

"Did the Wizard Watch send you?" Zora asked.

"No, no, heavens no, I'm not part of that ramble," the wizardly man said.

"You're Lord Hyrum the Sol," Jakoby said. "We met before, long ago, in the ceremonial chambers."

"Yes, Jakoby, I never forget an introduction." Hyrum shook the knight's shackled hand with both of his. He walked by the prisoners, inspecting each of them with probing eyes. He didn't say a word as he checked them over, from the boots on their feet to their hands and fingers. He got nose to nose in their faces.

Grey Cloak exchanged looks with Dyphestive and Zora. They shrugged. "Excuse me, Hyrum, but who are you?"

"I'm a Monarch." Without looking, he showed Grey Cloak the rings on his fingers. "See my signet ring, the onyx with a platinum crown? I'm royalty and also an enchanter as well as a diplomat, guild guider, and high giver."

"Oh," he said, his eyes fastened on the rings. The golden gem-studded jewelry reflected in his eyes. "Those rings are very nice. Do they do anything special?"

"Of course they do. That's interesting." Hyrum lifted Than's hands and rubbed his fingers. "Are these scales? Like a lizardman?"

"No," Than said.

"I always wished I had scales." Hyrum searched Than's eyes. "Not from this world, are you? Wooza! There seems to be a lot of that going around. It makes me wonder." He moved in front of Leena and waved his hand in front of her closed eyes. "The Ministry of Hoods. I like them. Very quiet people. This one's much cuter than the rest I've seen."

"Are you here to help us?" Grey Cloak asked curiously.

The older mage rubbed his face like he hadn't slept in days. "I wish I weren't, but I am. I have enough to deal with as it is. But I've been watching you. You intrigue me." He waved his hand at the ceiling.

Two rocky bulbs in the corners of the dungeon detached from the walls and sprouted wings. The yonders floated down to Hyrum.

"You've been spying on us?" Grey Cloak asked.

"And you should be glad I was. No one else wants to defend you, but based on what I've seen, I will. You're not innocent, by any means, but given your circumstances, it's possible the courts could be persuaded."

"You'll be our advocate?" Jakoby asked.

"No, but I'll sponsor your advocate." Hyrum massaged his cheeks for a moment and poked Grey Cloak's chest. "You'll have to find your own advocate. Do you have one?"

Grey Cloak shrugged.

"That's not a good answer. If you don't have an advocate, the Monarchs will appoint you one, but I don't recommend that. It's a very delicate case, and the Monarchs are determined to make examples of you. After all, you embarrassed the manure out of them, and they can't stand the thought of anyone chuckling behind their backs." Hyrum grinned. "Oh, the look on their faces when they learned that they had been duped by a pair of youths. It was glorious."

"Hyrum, what happens if we don't win?" Zora asked.

"There will be a sentencing. Most likely death. More than likely, you'll be fed to the moat monsters. The citizens really enjoy that." Hyrum scanned their dreary settings. "Or you'll be left here to rot, the same as my good man, Jakoby, said. As for finding an advocate, if you can think of anyone, I suggest you do it. And it better be a good one. I shall return." Hyrum walked straight between the bars, like a ghost. The yonders squeezed their eyeball bodies between the bars as well, fluttering their wings until they popped out on the other side.

"Can you at least give us some relief?" Zora shouted.

Hyrum winked at her. "I will." He walked down the hall and vanished around a corner.

"Who are we going to use for our advocate?" Grey Cloak asked. "Jakoby, do you know anybody?"

"I did, but no advocate within these walls would help me. I'd need an outsider, but I don't know anybody."

"What about Crane?" Dyphestive suggested.

"Is he an advocate?" Grey Cloak asked.

"I don't know, but he should be able to find one, shouldn't he?" Dyphestive asked.

Hyrum slid back in front of the bars. "Did you say Crane?"

"Yes," Grey Cloak replied.

"Funny, I've heard that name before. Where shall I fetch him?"

Grey Cloak told him where to find Crane.

"Excellent. Your fate is looking up." Hyrum looked down the dungeon hall and hollered, "Guard! Guard!"

Two Honor Guards in full scale armor appeared. The taller one carried a ring of keys. "Yes, Lord Hyrum of Sol."

"Take those chains off, and get these people something to eat. They're under my protection now."

The Honor Guard unlocked the door, and just as he pulled it open, a dark womanly voice said, "Not so fast."

34

"Elisha!" Hyrum said her name more like a disapproving gasp. "What are you doing here?"

The woman stepped into full view. Elisha was the skinniest elf Grey Cloak had ever seen, with skin so pale it was almost translucent. She had delicate but haunting features, and her head was smooth and bald. The midnight-blue dress she wore hung loosely from her body like a dry sheet. As haunting as she was, she was pretty, very pretty. She was escorted by four Honor Guards.

Grey Cloak's heart started pounding at the sight of the odd but captivating woman. His throat turned dry.

Elisha looked down her nose at Hyrum. "There's no time for pleasantries. They will all be heading to trial now."

"Now?" Hyrum balled his fists at his sides. "What's the

hurry, Elisha? Is this going to interfere with one of your hundred eighteen boorish dinner parties?"

"We're expecting company, and we don't want to be in the middle of these proceedings when they arrive," she said as she glanced at the prisoners from the corner of her eye. "They could arrive at any moment."

"The monarchy is always expecting company." He shook his fist at her. "That is all they do, entertain company. I'm sponsoring the accused, Elisha. And let me warn you that you are not to talk to them without me being present."

"No, I'm not to talk to them without their advocate being present." She stepped inside the cell. "You are not their advocate, but the court can certainly appoint one."

"No! I'll be back," Hyrum hollered at Grey Cloak. "Don't tell them anything!" He hurried down the hall.

Elisha stroked Grey Cloak's cheek with her slender fingers. "So, you're the mastermind behind the theft of Codd's shield. You're very... young. Impressive."

He felt her cool, minty breath on his face. Her dark, haunting eyes drew him in. He wanted to tell her everything about himself.

"Is there something that you wish to say?" Elisha turned her ear toward his lips. "I'm listening," she said seductively.

"Gum up, Grey Cloak," Zora said. Her eyes were boring a hole through Elisha. "Who are you?"

"The Monarchs' personal counsel. I've never lost a case

for them. I don't plan to either." Elisha stepped back and scanned their faces as she slowly rubbed her hands together. "The question is, shall I try you individually or as one? You're a group, are you not?"

"We are called Talon," Dyphestive innocently offered.

"Stifle it," Zora said.

"Talon," Elisha said as she drummed her long black fingernails on her shoulder. "It sounds threatening. I like it. If anyone would like to say anything else, even though I am opposing counsel, I can still be very persuasive to the courts. For instance, if you were to confess, your sentence would be lighter and painless." Four yonders flew into the cell and hovered behind her. "You can trust me. Tell me everything."

Grey Cloak found himself wrapped up in her hypnotic eyes. Her voice was so soft and soothing, like a purring animal. "I..."

"Yes?" she asked as he came closer. "Talk to me, Grey Cloak. Make this easy."

"Grey Cloak!" Zora shouted. "Don't say a word! She's trying to trick you! Get away from him! Get away —*mmmph!*"

With her eyes fixed on Grey Cloak, Elisha stuck her hand out and made a fist.

Zora's mouth clamped shut.

"You were saying?" Elisha encouraged.

He could feel her words pulling the thoughts from his

mind and down to his lips. Grey Cloak wanted to admit to everything. After all, his intentions were good, and the court would have to understand.

"Tell me what you're thinking, Grey Cloak," Elisha continued in her soothing voice. "Tell me, and everything will be fine. What happened? Did you steal the shield? Did you steal Codd's shield? Tell me, Grey Cloak. Tell me."

Grey Cloak's voice swam inside his mind, wanting to scream out everything inside. His lips parted. A guilty admission emerging.

A familiar voice cut him off. "Crane! Advocate Crane, that is!"

Crane eyed Elisha and looked her up and down approvingly. "And who might this enchantress be?"

Elisha's long neck slowly twisted. Her stare could have burned a hole straight through Crane and Hyrum. "How did you get him here so fast?"

"As it turns out, he was waiting by the drawbridge." Hyrum walked inside the cell and put his arm around her skinny waist. "We'll see you in the courtroom, Elisha."

Elisha stormed down the hall with her yonder and Honor Guard escorts hurrying along behind her.

"You didn't say anything, did you?" Hyrum asked as he motioned for the Honor Guard to give him the keys.

"No," Grey Cloak said, blinking heavily. His head swam. "She's very persuasive though. I wanted to tell her everything."

"Yes, Elisha is a veritable mistress of charisma. An enchanter, like me. It looks like we made it back in time," Hyrum said as the Honor Guard unchained the prisoners from the walls.

Zora was the first one to stretch out, groan, and take a seat on a damp bed of straw. She rubbed her ankles. "My legs were burning like fire. In a few more moments, I would have admitted to anything."

As the group wandered through the cell and stretched their aching limbs, Grey Cloak huddled with Crane and Hyrum. "Crane, I didn't know you were an advocate."

"I didn't either," Crane said with the same surprised expression. "But don't worry. I can handle this. I'm a good talker."

Grey Cloak rolled his eyes. "So, we don't have a true advocate, do we?"

"It seems so." Hyrum let out a raspy sigh. "Once we get into that courtroom, Elisha is going to eat us alive."

35

The courtroom was a majestically built rotunda made from smooth sections of pure marble. A dome of golden stained glass bathed the large chambers in warm light as the sun quavered high above.

At the front of the room, three judges wearing black robes sat behind a boxed-in dark-oak stand on a high stage. One woman sat between two men, an orc and an elf. All three had hard looks in their eyes, and their lips were drawn tight, like bowstrings.

To the left of the judges' stand was the witness stand, where Zora sat, wearing chains around her wrists and ankles. Her hair was messed up, her face still scratched and bruised.

Elisha asked questions, while Crane, Hyrum, Grey Cloak, Dyphestive, and the other members of Talon watched from their heavily guarded seats in front of the High Council.

Honor Guards in scale armor surrounded the room as well as many Monarch Knights in shiny platemail of the finest craft.

A circular balcony looked down on the main chamber floor. Every seat was filled with Monarchs, who wore the finest clothing, but their faces were covered with cowls or veils. The only other people in the room were the witnesses sitting behind Elisha, who she would call to the stand.

Elisha continued with her hard line of questioning. "Zora, when did Grey Cloak tell you that he wanted to steal Codd's shield?"

"Objection," Crane said. He sat with his hands on his belly, rolling his thumbs. "Counsel is insinuating that my clients had a plan, and they did not."

The woman judge frowned at Crane. "Overruled."

Crane winked at the judge. "Thank you, Mighty Councillor."

The judge turned her head away.

Zora continued, "Grey Cloak never mentioned anything to me about stealing the shield. I was being held for ransom by the Dark Addler. Stealing the shield was one of his terms for my release."

Elisha ran her fingers across the railing of the witness stand. "I see. So, it was either steal Codd's shield or assassinate members of the monarchy?"

"What?" Zora exclaimed.

Loud gasps filled the chamber.

Crane stood and put his knuckles on the table. "Objection. Counsel is putting words in my client's mouth. No one was attacked or killed. No one even mentioned anything about assassination."

"Overruled," the lady judge said.

Crane flopped down in his chair. "What sort of trial is this? They won't listen to common sense."

"Get used to it, but you're doing well for someone who hasn't been an advocate before," Hyrum assured him.

"My great-great-great-great-grandfather on my father's side was one. That's who I was named after," Crane proudly admitted. "I think I have a knack for this."

Grey Cloak leaned across Hyrum to Crane, who sat on the end. "We're getting slaughtered."

"Don't worry. I'll straighten this out when I cross-examine the witness," Crane said.

Grey Cloak leaned back in his seat and looked up at the dome. He imagined Cinder crashing through the glass, rescuing them, and setting all the fools of the monarchy on fire.

It's outrageous that I am sitting here, accused by these blind people. I'm a Sky Rider. A Sky Rider! One of the most powerful warriors in the world, and here I am, being judged by a bunch of wealthy fools. He scanned the crowd of hidden faces above him. *And for their amusement. What a shame!*

"High Councillors, my inquiry with this witness is concluded," Elisha said.

The judges on the High Council nodded.

Elisha took her seat at the table adjacent to the defendants and said, "Your witness," to Crane.

Crane stood and strutted across the courtroom with a warm smile on his face. He faced the judges. "May I please address the High Council?"

"No," a high councillor said. "Question your witness."

"But I believe we have a severe misunderstanding," Crane argued. "If I could only have a few moment—*ack!*"

A sliver of lightning shot out of a wand in one of the judges' hands.

Crane's back arched, and he rose on tiptoe, shaking uncontrollably.

"You will not speak freely to the High Council," the woman warned. She tapped the wand on the judges' stand.

Crane clung to the witness stand, gasping for breath. With his forehead beaded in sweat, he shuffled back to his seat. "No further questions."

THE NEXT HOUR WAS AGONY. Elisha carved up every witness she put on the stand and jabbed them with false allegations.

Crane objected to all of them but did so while ducking

underneath the table. Every one of his objections was over-ruled. So far, the defense had nothing to support their case.

Hyrum brought them into a huddle. "Listen to me. We've made it this far, so they are listening. Don't give Elisha what she wants. She wants you to look guilty. Don't act guilty. You aren't guilty. You're heroes. Keep your chins up, and act like it."

After Talon and their advocates huddled, Elisha called her next witness. "The people of Monarch Castle call Grey Cloak to the stand."

Grey Cloak shuffled toward the witness stand with his chains dragging behind him. He winked at Elisha and sat.

Elisha didn't bat an eye as she ran her slender hand over the smooth skin of her bald head. "For the record, state your name for the court."

"Grey Cloak."

"Interesting, so your mother named you after a garment?"

The court rotunda filled with chuckles.

"Order, order," the leader of the High Council said.

The room fell silent.

"I never knew my mother. I was an orphan, so I named myself," he said.

Elisha rolled her eyes. "I see. An orphan with a habit of stealing. Grey Cloak, tell the court why you stole Codd's shield."

"I'd be glad too." He managed a smile. "You see, my

friend Zora"—he pointed to her—"was taken hostage by Irsk Mondo, the leader of the Dark Addler. He wanted Codd's shield in exchange for her freedom. He said that he would kill her or sell her into slavery. I had to do something."

Elisha paced away with her hands behind her back. "That's interesting. Very interesting. Have you lived in Monarch City very long, Grey Cloak?"

He shrugged. "Only about a year."

"That's not very long. But you've lived here long enough to hear rumors of a secret society called the Dark Addler?"

"Secret society?" He raised his voice. "You must have seen the Iron Devils we fought in the sun gods' cathedral. What could explain their presence besides the Dark Addler?"

The head councillor tapped her wand on her stand and pointed it at him. "No more outbursts."

"Thank you, High Councillor." Elisha sauntered in front of the judges' stand. "If it pleases the court, I would like to bring in the man in question, Irsk Mondo."

"I'll allow it," the judge said.

Elisha pointed to the doors in the back of the room. An Honor Guard opened the large brass doors, and Irsk Mondo entered in a wheelchair pushed by Finton Slay.

Grey Cloak's stomach dropped to his feet.

Zooks!

Finton Slay pushed Irsk Mondo down the aisle in his rickety chair with squeaky wheels. Irsk crouched in the chair. His arm was in a sling, and he had a heavy blanket covering his knees. With his swollen face, he looked pitiful. His skinny fingers stroked the Scarf of Shadows.

"I object!" Crane said as he cowered behind his chair.

"What are you objecting to?" the councillor asked.

"I didn't know about this witness."

"You didn't know about any of them. You were poorly prepared," the high councillor said.

"But none of us—"

The high councillor waggled her wand.

Crane deflated as he sat down.

"High Councillor, the prosecution would like to call a new witness," Elisha said with a smug look.

"The witness is dismissed," the high councillor said to Grey Cloak.

Grey Cloak returned to his seat with his shoulders slumped. He glared at Irsk the entire way, but his stare wasn't half as hot as Zora's. She had murder in her eyes.

"I would like to call Irsk Mondo to the stand," Elisha said with a sympathetic look in her eyes.

"If only I were able," Irsk replied feebly.

The chamber was filled with a chorus of sympathetic "aws."

"You can provide witness for us from where you sit, Irsk Mondo," the high councillor said. "We thank you for your courage to even come here. Please, continue, prosecutor."

"Thank you, High Councillor." Elisha nodded at Finton Slay, and he took a seat at the prosecutor's table. "For the record, what is your name?"

"Irsk Mondo."

"Tell us a little bit about yourself, if you will."

"Objection," Crane said. He caught a frosty look and sat down. "Never mind."

"I've lived in Monarch City most of my life. I was an orphan, not that that was so bad, but what was bad was being an orphan who was part elf and part goblin." Irsk shivered in his chair. "The horrible things that the other children would say about me. And the adults too. Life was hard on me."

Grey Cloak looked up at the sobbing people. He couldn't believe his eyes and ears. He caught Dyphestive sniffling and elbowed him.

"What did you do that for?" Dyphestive whispered.

"You don't believe this, do you?"

"I don't know what to believe. It all sounds so good."

Grey Cloak slapped his face.

I'm starting to wonder what I believe. She's starting to confuse me.

"Well, I learned at a very young age to always treat others with kindness, no matter how poorly they treated me," Irsk said as he rocked back and forth and coughed from time to time. "You see, I was raised by some very kind women in the orphanage. They took care of me, and over time, I came to take care of them when they were in need. They were all so very sweet, and I felt that I owed it to them to carry on with their work and take care of the orphans in Monarch City and find them good homes." He coughed. "It is my passion."

"I think that most of us here are well aware of your contributions to the abandoned children in this city. I for one would like to thank you for your great efforts," Elisha said.

The chamber broke out in applause.

The high councillor tapped her wand on the stand. "Order. Order. As much as we'd like to commend Irsk Mondo's achievements, it's more important that we carry on with these proceedings without further distraction. Please continue, Advocate."

Elisha pointed at Grey Cloak's table. "Irsk, do you know these people?"

Irsk wheeled his chair around to face the table. It squeaked as he did so. He squinted his eyes. "I don't know all of them, but yes, I've seen them before."

"But do you *know* them? Like friends or in business?" she asked.

"No, the first time I ever saw them was yesterday when I was worshipping at the cathedral." He pointed at Grey Cloak. "He was in an awful rush, and I asked him if I could assist them. That was when I noticed Codd's shield. I've been to the crypt many times before. I take the orphans there, as they so enjoy it." His jaw tightened. "That's when I confronted these thieves! These cowards! They tried to kill me, a cripple, for it."

"Cripple my arse!" Zora jumped up and screamed. "He's a liar! He's a filthy rotten liar!"

"Remove her!" the high councillor ordered.

Honor Guards dragged Zora, kicking and screaming, from the court chamber. Zora cursed Irsk Mondo the entire way.

"If anyone else behaves like that, the punishment will be swift and painful." The high councillor pointed her wand at Crane. "Very painful." She gave Irsk a sad look. "Please, continue."

"Well, there isn't much more to say. I did my best to fight them off, but there were so many, they simply overwhelmed me. Some brave parishioners, however, fought against them. I believe a few died in the process." Irsk let out a long, wheezing sigh. "All of this in the house of the sun gods. Such a blasphemous event to occur in a sanctuary well-known for spreading peace. I am so glad that the horrific event is behind us and that I can be a witness to justice and help see that these rogues are put in their place."

Silence fell over the rotunda.

Talon's members' shoulders slumped, and their faces were blank. They were all being cornered with lies and deceit, and the Monarchs were a party to it all.

Elisha broke the quiet. "I don't have any further questions, High Councillor."

Crane stood. "I do."

The high councillor narrowed her eyes. "Irsk Mondo has been through enough. Have a seat, Advocate. It's time for closing arguments." She tapped her wand on the stand. "We'll take a short recess."

There was no mistaking the subtle smile on Irsk Mondo's face as Finton Slay wheeled him out of the rotunda. He winked at Grey Cloak on the way out, blew a kiss at the others, and waved a final goodbye.

Crane brushed his hands over his brass-button coat. "Well, at least I get to have a closing argument."

"It better be a good one," Hyrum said.

37

Elisha stood directly in front of the three judges, who looked down on her from the stand with heavy eyes. She cleared her throat. "A great crime has been committed against the monarchy. Not just the Monarchs themselves, but the entire city that they protect. Why? Because of thieves—greedy, self-centered, cold, heartless, murdering thieves."

She spun on her heel, smoothed her hand over her bald head, and faced the accused.

"Look at them, High Councillors. Hard-faced, dirty, and with innocent blood on their hands. They taint this very courtroom with their vile presence." Elisha sneered at them. "Who do they think they are? They plan and scheme to take your, our, historical treasure. The very shield of Codd himself. A symbol of freedom, liberty, hard work, and sacrifice. What would compel them to do this?"

She faced the High Council.

"They will try to convince you of a wild tale about how they didn't have a choice. That they were blackmailed. By who? Irsk Mondo, one of the most, if not the most, benevolent citizens in this entire city. They accused him of being the mastermind behind the Dark Addler, a secret society that rules Monarch City's devious underbelly." She laughed. "It's outrageous."

She approached the bench and looked each of them directly in the eye. The high councillors leaned in, hanging on her every word.

"Monarch City cannot stand for this crime. It cannot show mercy to these thieves. We would be the laughing-stock of all nine territories for letting a pack of mangy curs get away with a crime like this. And what about Codd? Yes, Codd himself, who fought so hard, so valiantly, to create a foundation of safety. What about his sacrifice? The sacrifice he and his brave knights made to boldly carve our future by shedding their blood. Is this what those men died for? They died so that the hard-working, benevolent, kind, generous, and loving Monarchs of this fair city could be robbed by the very face of evil?"

Elisha turned and pointed at Talon. "Those men and women are the face of evil. They are the face of everything Codd stood against, everything that he died to prevent. His bravery brought order to a wild territory and made it a haven for all who are good in this world, and these rodents came to steal that away."

She faced the High Council once more. "Talon. That is what they call themselves. A talon is a weapon." She made a claw with her hand and held it up. "It is a weapon used to tear flesh from the bone. To rip the heart out of its prey so the predator can feed on it." Elisha slashed her hand through the air twice.

The audience gasped.

"I warn you if you don't declaw or destroy this Talon, there will be more. There will be more." She nodded to the High Council, turned, and quietly walked back to her table, her heels echoing on the floor.

"Blood horseshoes," Dyphestive said under his breath. "Even I feel guilty."

Grey Cloak's throat tightened. They didn't stand a chance unless Crane pulled off some sort of miracle. He eyed the glass-domed ceiling, hoping the Sky Riders would drop in and save the day. It didn't happen. It was all up to a tubby, wizened fellow named Crane, who had his eyes closed and fingers locked over his belly. The man was snoring.

We're doomed.

38

The leader of the High Council rapped her wand on the bench. "Advocate Crane," she said in an irritated voice. "Advocate Crane!"

Hyrum nudged Crane.

Crane's eyes popped open, and he wiped drool from the corner of his mouth onto his sleeve. "Is it my turn?"

"Yes," Hyrum said. "What were you doing?"

"Meditating." Crane rose. "She's really going to let me speak?"

"She always does. You have to persuade two councillors, Crane," Hyrum urged him. "I believe you can do it."

Crane lifted his brows. "I didn't think she would let me, or I would have prepared something." He saw everyone's heads drop. "Oh well, it's go time."

"Hurry up, Advocate Crane. The High Council has more than one case to review today."

"Of course." Crane walked right up to the bench and rested his arm on it. "This is a beautiful, just beautiful, rotunda. I've been all over the world, and I have never seen one so grand." He ran his hand over the lacquered finish of the dark wood and looked at the leader of the High Council. "I bet your skin is this smooth."

She pointed the wand at him. "Be careful what you say, Advocate Crane. This court does not cater to flattery."

"No, of course not. My apologies." He stepped away from the bench, spread his arms wide, and backed up. "Flattery. Monarch City is full of flattery. Everyone is always patting each other or themselves on the back, saying how perfect they are. How perfect Monarch City is. Why, it is perfect." He spun around in a full circle and pointed at Elisha. "Or is it?"

Crane walked as he talked, with his arms swinging at his sides, in a slow gait.

"Everything that Monarch City's advocate has said is pure bunk. A lie. Not true. All she has done is build a wall that is no thicker than the hairs on her head. That's right. She's lovely but bald, and so is her case against Talon. It's all a bald-faced lie."

The audience sat on the edge of their seats. Many leaned over the railing.

"Monarch City, its citizens, say that they want the truth.

Well, if you want the truth, if you want justice, then you need to listen." He pointed to Talon. "These men and women are heroes, heroes fashioned from the same mold as Codd himself. That's right. Their friend was taken captive. She was starved, beaten, and tortured by the very same Dark Addler that you claim exists, but when it's right in front of your face, you deny it.

"I want you to ask yourself this. What would Codd do if an innocent woman, a friend, or a family member was taken against her will? Would Codd stand around and do nothing, or would he do everything in his power to save her? Would he give up his shield to save her, or his, life? You know the answer to that. You know he would." Crane's voice was strong and compelling.

"Codd saves lives. Plain and simple. Why, he is the very inspiration for heroic men and women such as the members of Talon. They do good because they feel compelled to. They risk their very lives to fight for what is right."

He faced Talon. "Look at them, battered and bruised. Those are the faces of people who fight the good fight. Those are the faces of people willing to make a sacrifice. If you are going to face evil, then you're going to get your hands dirty. Isn't that what Codd said? Fighting for good is a bloody business! That is what he said."

He ran his meaty hand over his jaw.

"My, what would Codd think if he were here? Don't

you think that he would sniff out the truth? Don't you think he'd see right through the veil of lies and deceit?" He looked right at the High Council. "We all know he would.

"Yes, a crime was committed. It was committed right here in this courtroom, where a villain was glorified and these heroes were smeared." He shook his head. "I am hurt, wounded, saddened, and ashamed. How can the monarchy be so blind?

"Well, whether it comes today or tomorrow or years from now, we all know this: the truth will come out. And when the truth does come out, will this court be found on the side of truth, on the side of Codd, or will it be on the other side of the flaming fence?"

Crane patted the judges' stand. "The truth will come out." He returned to his seat.

Elisha sat quietly with her face drawn tight. The dark-eyed woman nodded at Crane. Grey Cloak reached behind Hyrum and patted Crane on the back. Dyphestive's face glowed.

The citizens in the balcony murmured, but the high councillor quieted them down with a tap of her wand. "Order. Order. The High Council will deliberate and return with a decision." She stood and stepped down from the bench, and the other two High Council members followed her out of the chamber.

Hyrum rubbed Crane's shoulders. "You did fantastic!

Wooza! You definitely bent their ears and gave us a chance."

"Now what?" Grey Cloak asked. All the members of Talon crowded behind his back. "How long does it take them to deliberate?"

"Maybe an hour or so. Sometimes it can take days. If that's the case, you'll have to wait in the dungeon," Hyrum said. "Wooza, you really stuck it to Elisha. I could hear her rear end pucker when you called her out. I've never seen anyone get the best of her, but you did."

Crane gave a clever smile. "I did, didn't I?"

"What happens if we win?" Dyphestive asked.

"If the High Council rules in your favor, because they tried you all as one, you will be set free immediately."

"Even me?" Jakoby asked.

"Yes, you'll be cleared of all accusations."

Jakoby pumped his fist. "Yes."

The lizardman bailiff standing near the door to the High Council's private chambers said, "All arise!"

Everyone in the courtroom stood as the high councillors entered and took their seats behind the bench.

"That was fast," Grey Cloak said. "Wasn't it?"

"That was too fast," Hyrum replied.

Grey Cloak glanced at Elisha. She had a confident look in her eyes. She offered him a subtle nod that made his skin prickle.

"Sit," the leader of the High Council said. "During our

deliberation, the High Council made a unanimous decision. The party that calls itself Talon has been found guilty of theft, treason, wanton endangerment, public menace, and lying under oath. Sentencing will follow immediately. Guard, see to it that this rabble is firmly secured."

39

In stunned silence, Talon remained standing as they listened to the verdict.

"All members of Talon will be executed by hanging as soon as the gallows are erected." The leader of the High Council's eyes swept through the room and locked on Sergeant Tinison, who stood near the front. "Notify the high executioner immediately, Sergeant. In the meantime, remove the accused from this council room to the appropriate holding chambers."

Sergeant Tinison nodded. "Right away, High Councillor."

As the High Council departed for their chambers, Elisha passed by the company and offered her hand to Crane. "Well done, for a novice advocate. You actually gave me a shred of doubt, which I haven't felt in a long time."

Crane kissed her hand. "Perhaps we can talk more over dinner."

"Perhaps." Elisha waved goodbye and walked away.

"Well, don't let us get in the way of your dinner plans, Crane," Grey cloak said. "Be sure to dine on a balcony where you can get a full view of us hanging."

Crane's mouth opened in an *o*. "I'd never do something like that. It would make the lady uncomfortable."

Grey Cloak bull-rushed Crane. Several Honor Guards pulled him back. "Whose side are you on anyway?"

"I tried my best. I'm sure you'll think of something," Crane said. He grabbed his leather satchel and stuffed his notes inside. "If you'll excuse me, I have to make plans for dinner before she gets away."

Honor Guards escorted Talon to the holding cells in a lockup just outside the courtroom. Gray clouds rolled across a bleak skyline. Everyone slogged along, their chains dragging behind them.

Zora sat on a bench in the cell with her shoulders leaning against the wall. Her bottom lip stuck out, and her cheeks were red. "Let me guess. We lost."

Grey Cloak slumped beside her as an Honor Guard locked them all in the same cell. "You're a good guesser. Care to guess what our sentence is?"

"Does it matter?" she asked. "I knew I was dead the moment I came in here. Monarchs, dirty, rotten, filthy Monarchs. I thought they were supposed to be good."

"They're a mixed lot," Jakoby said as he stared out the barred prison window. "I really thought for a moment that Crane had pulled it off. He gave me hope, even after Elisha spewed her sea of lies. I don't know how people live with themselves."

Dyphestive was leaning against the steel bars sealing them in the cell when Hyrum approached.

"I'm sorry. Very sorry," Hyrum said as he wiped his sea-green sleeve over his eyes. "Even for my kind, this is extreme, and I'm not sure what's driving it. Of course, I've been on the outside a long time. The monarchy has become a hard nut to crack. Wooza. I bet Elisha knows something. Perhaps Crane can get something out of her before they get the gallows built."

"Well, he better talk fast because the gallows are halfway up," Jakoby said.

Grey Cloak approached the window. A group of Honor Guards were lifting posts, setting them in the ground, and hammering pegs into the long timbers. Every loud hit sent a tingle down his spine.

I'm going to have to figure out a way out of here.

Soldiers stood all over the castle's courtyards and paced the walls. Nothing but open ground stretched between the castle and the drawbridge. They would all be shot down by a thousand arrows before they made it halfway. Not to mention, he had no desire to hurt anybody.

He approached Hyrum. "If you know a way out of here, now is the time to spill it."

"Their eyes are everywhere," Hyrum said. "I have powers but not enough to overcome this. I'll do what I can to stall. I'm fairly good at talking." He left, and a pair of Honor Guards entered.

"Jakoby," Sergeant Tinison said. "Someone would like to speak to you before your time in Gapoli ends."

"Beak!" Dyphestive exclaimed as he pressed his face to the bars. "It's good to see you."

"Don't talk to me, you traitor. You are going to get what's coming to you," Beak said bitterly.

"But I had to, and you would have done the same thing," Dyphestive stated.

Beak turned away from Dyphestive and faced Jakoby. She stuck her hands through the bars and clasped his. "Uncle, I don't want to see you go. Not like this. Not without honor. Tell me why."

"You wouldn't understand. I was betrayed, the same as my brother, your father," Jakoby said with watery eyes.

"The Doom Riders killed my father, not the Monarch Knights. They would never do that. They would never betray their oaths," she said.

"A wise man told me that oaths are made to be broken," Jakoby said. "That was your father, Adanadel."

Her jaw dropped open. "Why would he say that?"

"He didn't say it because he didn't believe in the oath

and what it stood for. He said it because men are not perfect. Your father understood that. We all strive for a higher standard, but we all make mistakes. Our words can be turned against us." He glanced back at the company. "These are good people. They risked everything to do the right thing. They sacrificed their lives for each other. That is the truth, Shannon." He stroked her cheek. "Remember that."

"I know what I saw," she said with a sideways glance at Dyphestive. "He helped steal Codd's shield."

"Your judgment cannot be so rigid. Tell her, Dyphestive," Jakoby said.

"Tell me what?" she asked.

Shamefaced and using a soft tone, Dyphestive said, "I'm the reason your father died."

40

"What is this?" Beak's face turned red. "I'm in no mood for games. My father was killed by the Doom Riders. I was told this. Is that a lie too?"

"No, Beak, I mean Shannon, it's true. I swear it," Dyphestive said. "And I'm not proud of it. It happened when your father was trying to save us."

"Why would he be trying to save you?" she asked.

"Because—"

Grey Cloak cut Dyphestive off. "Because the Doom Riders came after us. They had a bounty on our heads. It's a long story, and it doesn't look like we have time to get into the details. But the Doom Riders killed your father and many others that night in Raven Cliff. And we aren't finished with them yet."

"I don't believe you." Beak wiped a tear running down her cheek.

Zora came forward. "It's true. I was there, too, and witnessed three of my closest friends die. Dalsay, Browning, and Adanadel." She clutched the bars. "I know your pain, but you need to know the truth. Your father would only have given his life for a good cause."

Tears streamed down Shannon's cheeks. With a sob, she turned to Dyphestive. "Why didn't you tell me before?"

"I was going to when the right time came." He wrapped his big hand over her fist. "I'm sorry."

She sniffled. "If my father gave his life for you, then I know that there is good in you. But I want to know why. Why did the Doom Riders come for you?"

"I would like to know that myself," Sergeant Tinison asked. He narrowed his eyes at Grey Cloak and Dyphestive. "What is so special about you two?"

"It's a long story," Grey Cloak said as he grabbed Dyphestive by the wrist and squeezed. He could tell that his brother was about to blurt out everything, but he didn't want to reveal everything. Telling their enemy who they were could be used against them. He thought fast and said, "If you want to know the truth, you'll have to seek out the Wizard Watch after our deaths. Talon," he said as he looked at Beak, "worked with them. Ask for Tatiana."

"That's all? I must live with my father's demise

shrouded in mystery?" Shannon wiped the last tear from her eye. "I'm disappointed. I'm disappointed with all of you!" She stormed away.

Sergeant Tinison remained. He said to Jakoby, "I'll look after her." His eyes scanned the bars. "Looks like you have enough to worry about as it is." He looked at Grey Cloak and Dyphestive. "I have to admit, I'm curious what all of this is really about. It's a shame I won't find out. After all, duty calls. I'm sorry it didn't work out for you, Baby Face. Hopefully it will in the next life."

The members of Talon took turns looking out the window to watch the gallows being erected. The soldiers were hammering down the floor of the platform. A bearish bare-chested orc wearing a loose black hood carried a coil of rope in his thick arms. He carried the armful to the top of the platform. Sweat glistened between the patches of hair on his shoulders and chest as he spooled the rope into the shape of a noose.

"They're going to need a lot of rope to hang all of us," Jakoby said dryly as sweat trickled down his temple. "It looks like they have plenty."

"We have to find a way out of this," Grey Cloak said.

Than sat silently on the end of the cell's bench.

"Well, hermit from another world, don't you have anything to offer? Certainly, a man who's lived a thousand years has gotten himself out of predicaments worse than this before."

"This old hermit isn't what he used to be. I don't see an easy way out of this without killing or harming a large group of people severely," Than said as he brushed his long strands of hair away from his eyes. "I'm thinking."

"Well, think faster!" Zora said. She paced the cell with her eyebrows knitted. "These Monarchs really are something. We're going to die, and we didn't even kill anyone aside from the Iron Devils. Why weren't they brought up in all of this? And Irsk Mondo, that vermin, flaunting my scarf right before my eyes. He comes out smelling like a rose while sitting on a stinking pile of lies. I don't care who gets hurt. These people deserve it. It's us against them, and we have to do whatever it takes to save ourselves."

Leena stood beside Zora, crossed her arms, and nodded.

"Fine, Zora, I'm convinced. We're going to have to make a run for it the first chance we get," Grey Cloak said. "The way I see it, if we're going to die anyway, we might as well die fighting. Hopefully, some of us will escape."

Jakoby lifted his chains. "We won't get far in these shackles."

"No, but they'll take them off before we hang, I would think," Grey Cloak said. "That should give me the freedom I need." He moved back to the cell window. Outside, the burly orc tossed the nooses over the support beam.

Jakoby stood beside Grey Cloak. "That's the high executioner. Though many have tried, no one has ever escaped the grip of the gallows." He put a hand on Grey Cloak's shoulder. "At least in my lifetime."

41

A chill came with the darkening sky as Talon was led to the gallows. They snaked through the corridors and out to the courtyard, surrounded by the watchful eyes of the Honor Guard and the Monarch Knights. Every one of the Honor Guard had a spear in hand, and the Monarch Knights—towering men—looked on with hardened stares.

Grey Cloak glanced up. The clouds began to spit cold rain. He could have sworn he saw a dragon wing passing through the clouds. The soldiers shoved him along to the base of the gallows. He was followed by Dyphestive, Jakoby, Than, Zora, and Leena. Honor Guards removed their shackles while other members pointed spears at them.

Over one hundred members of the Honor Guard and Monarch Knights filled the small courtyard set aside for the gallows. It was a private area surrounded by ten-foot-high walls separating it from the rest of the castle. The castle's terraces and spired towers overlooked the courtyard, and the unfamiliar faces of the monarchy filled their windows. Others leaned over the balconies, sipping wine and talking quietly.

As Grey Cloak's hands were bound, he said to his brother, "I don't suppose you have any of that flying potion left on you?"

"Hah. I wish. Listen, brother, I don't blame you for this. You did your best. We did our best," Dyphestive said with a long face. "I am proud of you."

The words moved Grey Cloak's heart. "I'm proud of you too."

"Be silent!" Sergeant Tinison said. "You had plenty of time to say your goodbyes in the cell."

Dyphestive looked down at Sergeant Tinison. "What are you going to do, kill us?"

Sergeant Tinison fought back a smile. "Keep moving, losers."

Grey Cloak was the first one up the steps of the boxed-in stage. At the top, six nooses made from stiff rope swayed against the wind. He walked across the groaning stage and looked down. A drop floor below them creaked under their weight. He stood underneath his noose and ran his gaze along the rope. *This is going to hurt.*

The rest of Talon joined him on the stage.

One by one, the high executioner lowered the nooses

and tightened them around their necks. It started on the far end with Leena and finished with Grey Cloak. He could feel the abrasive rope burning into his skin. It became hard to swallow, not to mention the high executioner stank badly. "Do you bathe between executions? Or bathe at all, for that matter?"

The high executioner went about his business, tugging on the ropes and seeing to it that they were secure around everyone's necks.

"I'm not ashamed to say it, but I'm scared," Zora said with a sob. "I never thought I'd die. Not this way. I don't deserve this."

"None of us do," Jakoby said. "Especially you."

"I'm sorry, Zora. I'm sorry, everybody," Grey Cloak said. He scanned the faces in the crowd high and low. He didn't see Crane or anyone else that he knew. The faces of the soldiers were hardened. After all, he had embarrassed them. Beak's expression was the only exception. Her face was long, and she couldn't keep eye contact. He kept look-ing. *Crane, you have to be doing something. And where is Hyrum?*

The soldiers parted in the middle as a woman in a long black gown made her way to the gallows. It was the leader of the High Council, whose name had never been said. Her black robes hid her toes as she headed up the stairs of the gallows and stood on the platform beside the high executioner.

The high councillor spoke, and the low talking diminished. "Today, vermin will be removed from our ranks. Today, we set an example for all society. Today is the day that the wicked will taste the swift sting of justice. Today." She turned and faced the accused. "There will be no speeches, no apologies, and no mercy." She nodded at the high executioner.

The high executioner grabbed the lever.

Grey Cloak summoned his wizardry into his hands, which were tied behind his back.

It's now or never.

Without an object to channel the wizard fire into, his fingers started to burn.

The high councillor gave the high executioner another nod. He pulled the lever.

The floor dropped. Talon dropped. Grey Cloak dropped.

I'm too late!

42

I'm too late! Grey Cloak thought as the floor fell out from under him. He waited for the painful snap of his neck. His feet hit the ground instead. He glanced up. He saw all the members of Talon hanging, including himself, but when he turned his head, they were on the ground with him, and they weren't alone.

A handsome fellow with a razor-sharp dagger was sawing through their ropes. It was Reginald the Razor. "Don't stand there gawking," Reginald whispered. "Climb down into that tunnel, and get moving."

"But how?" Grey Cloak asked as he loosened the bindings around his hands. Up top, Talon was still hanging by their necks while the high councillor watched. He felt an icy touch on his arm and turned. "Tatiana?"

The gorgeous elven sorceress stood with the Star of

Light burning in her fingers. Her eyes glowed with starlight. "Wonderful memory. Make haste. My illusion will not fool them much longer."

Talon stood inside the boxed-in stage, hidden from the soldiers, with shocked looks on their faces. Then without hesitation, they vanished into the gap like a rabbit into its hole.

Grey Cloak watched above as a puzzled look grew on the high councillor's face. "I think she's onto us," he said as he swung his legs over the hole.

Yonders gathered above the stage, eyeballing the hanging group.

"We need to go," Reginald urged as he pushed Grey Cloak into the hole. "Go! Go! Come on, Tatiana."

Tatiana jumped down into the drainage tunnel.

The black-clad Razor pulled the grate closed. "We need to run."

The corner of Tatiana's mouth turned up. "One last thing."

THE HIGH COUNCILLOR studied the men and women hanging from the ropes. Her head tilted to the side when the yonders arrived and began flying around the bodies. Her facial features tightened as her gaze dropped. She leaned over the gap, and her eyes widened as a middling dragon erupted from beneath the stage.

"Dragon! Dragon!" the crowd of soldiers hollered as they drew their weapons.

The high executioner dove from the stage, and the high councillor fell backward off it. With the Monarchs shouting in horror at the tops of their lungs, the entire stage buckled and collapsed. The terrifying dragon flew into the sky, chased the yonders away with fire, and slowly vanished.

Down on the ground, Beak exchanged a bewildered look with Sergeant Tinison. He helped the high councillor to her feet. He dusted off her bottom, drawing a sour look from her, and backed away. The shaken woman quickly departed.

Under the sergeant's command, the Honor Guard slowly began picking up the collapsed stage.

They lifted plank after plank, searching for the hanged prisoners inside the wreckage. They didn't find a single body. Beak caught her breath. Talon was gone. A grin flashed over Sergeant Tinison's face as he gave Beak a subtle shrug. He addressed his men, "It looks like a dragon ate the bodies. Haven't we chased all those dragons out of the sewers yet?"

43

Talon scurried through the drainage tunnels underneath Castle Monarch, where they came to a stop at a junction.

"Now what?" Grey Cloak asked as the drainage water trickled over his toes.

"We wait," Tatiana said. The gemstone in her hand offered the only source of light in the darkness.

"Wait for what? They're going to find us down here," he said.

"The only way out of the city is to cross the drawbridge or fly," Jakoby commented. "Unless you can traverse the moat and stay the hunger of the monsters."

Tatiana opened her mouth to speak, but Zora crashed into her. She wrapped the sorceress in a strong hug. "Thank you! Thank you! Thank you! And I missed you!"

"I missed you, too, little sister," Tatiana said as she petted Zora's head and hugged her back. "All is well now, for the moment."

Dyphestive joined in the hug. "Thank you."

"Thanks from all of us, but we need to keep moving," Grey Cloak said. "We can celebrate later, but only if there is a later. Tatiana, you found a way in here, so where is the way out?"

"The same way we came in, over the drawbridge." Tatiana's eyes swept over the stone ceiling of the pipe. "I'd advise you all to keep your voices down. The tunnels will carry sound to the grates in the streets. Follow me."

Talon followed the sorceress from the Wizard Watch without another word. They passed one intersection after another and moved deeper below the surface.

The air became stagnant and rank. They stopped at an intersection where the waters gathered at the bottom. Everyone took a moment to catch their breaths.

"I never thought the stink of the sewers would smell so sweet," Jakoby said with his hands on his knees. "I thought we were finished when he put that noose around my neck." He looked at Tatiana. "Lady, you have my gratitude." He switched his gaze to Reginald the Razor. "You too." He offered his hand. "That's a lot of steel you're packing."

"This is my lighter set," Reginald said with a grin. The energetic youth's brown hair swooshed across the top of his eyebrows. He was dressed in black leather armor. Sharp-edged weapons, some sheathed, some not, decorated his body. A pair of longswords crisscrossed his back, and short swords hung from his hips. A bandolier of knives crossed his chest, and daggers adorned his belt and legs. He had leather bracers, too, with small blades tucked inside. He unsheathed a longsword and handed it to Jakoby. "Take it. Anyone else who needs some steel, help yourself." He raised a finger. "But if you lose it, you buy it."

Zora helped herself to a pair of daggers from his bandolier. Leena eyed Razor up and down and took a short sword.

"What about you, old fella?" Razor asked Than. "Can I help you out as well?"

Than exposed his long fingernails. "These will do."

Razor's lips curled. "Uh, sure, even if it's creepy."

"Is there a way down to get out of here, or do we have to go back up?" Grey Cloak asked.

"I don't think there's another way across the moat. Or at least I'm not aware of one. Using the drainage pipes was only part of the plan." Tatiana smiled. "Be patient."

"They'll send hounds into the sewers," Jakoby said.

"Not if they think that you're dead," Tatiana said. "That was the reason for my illusion. The Brotherhood of Whispers works above in your favor. It has faces that work behind the scenes."

"Is Tanlin here?" Zora asked hopefully.

"No. It's best to assume that he's home safe in Raven

Cliff, a far safer place than here," Tatiana said as she watched the ceiling.

"What do you mean, Tatiana?" Grey Cloak asked as he looked at the grim expression on her face. "What is it that you aren't telling us?"

The tunnel quaked. Centuries of grit dropped from the crusty ceiling. The tunnel quaked again. Everyone hunkered down, the whites of their eyes showing in the dark.

"Tatiana," Grey Cloak said with growing concern. "What is going on?"

She faced them. "Black Frost is invading."

44

As the ground trembled above them, Grey Cloak ran up the tunnel and climbed through a smaller pipe to a street grate. The courtyard was burning. Soldiers barked orders over terrified screams. A wave of flames washed over the walkways and set the gardens on fire as a middling dragon raced by.

"Riskers!" Grey Cloak said as he dropped back into the tunnel. "It's true!"

"Now is the time to make our escape," Tatiana said. "Follow me!"

"Wait, you knew about this?" Grey Cloak asked.

"The Wizard Watch keeps a close eye on Black Frost's dealings," she said as she made her way up the tunnel.

Grey Cloak grabbed her by her long ponytail and pulled her back. "Hold your horses, Tat! If the Wizard

Watch knew about this, why didn't they warn the Monarchs?"

She gave him a heavy look. "We did."

"Disgraceful!" Jakoby spit. "How can the Monarchs do this? Men and women will be slaughtered up there."

"Not if they surrender," she said.

"The Monarchs will never surrender," Jakoby argued.

"Then they'll die."

Grey Cloak didn't waste any more time. He ran up the tunnel and didn't stop until the pipe opened into a storm drain running beneath the castle's walls. He stood against the wall and watched the chaos unfold.

Riskers and their dragons crisscrossed the sky. There were dozens of them, grand dragons and middling dragons alike. The Riskers rode on their backs, wearing suits of blackened platemail armor. Many of them had glowing dragon charms mounted in their chest plates. They passed over the castle's grounds like gusts of wind, spewing white-hot fire from their mouths.

The courtyards, the gardens, the storehouses burned. Black smoke carried over the walls toward the city. On the ground and on the walls, the Honor Guard and Monarch Knights were fighting for their lives and the lives of others.

A squad of twelve dragons streaked over the walls and dropped out of sight into the city. The cries of the citizens could be heard across the moat on the other side of the wall.

"They're everywhere," Jakoby said as he followed the trail of dragons flying through the skies, dropping down, and setting the world on fire. "Everywhere!"

The soldiers manning the towers fired their ballistae at the dragons. The long shafts of metal flew true to their marks, piercing one middling dragon through the neck and blasting a Risker out of the saddle.

A grand dragon swept up from the moat, hovered in the air, his wings beating, and set the tower on fire. Burning men jumped from the tower and crashed to the ground at the base of the wall.

Honor Guard foot soldiers pushed catapults across the grounds. They loaded massive nets into the scoops, pulled back the triggers, and sent the nets spinning skyward. The nets tangled up a middling dragon's wings. It spiraled out of control and nose-dived to the ground.

A Risker crawled away from the wreckage with a glowing sword in her hands.

The Honor Guard cut her down with swords and pierced the dragon with spears. They looked up just in time to see a dragon come roaring right at them. It set the Honor Guards on fire and destroyed a catapult with a single breath.

On the wall above them, the Monarch Knights bravely hurled spears and javelins into the sky. A grand dragon flew right at them with a geyser of flame spewing from its mouth. The top of that section of wall exploded into flame.

Burning bodies flew over the side and hit the ground with jarring impact.

One knight rose to a knee with his sword in hand and his armor smoking. Another one didn't move. The knight with smoking armor exchanged a look with Talon, adjusted his helmet, and headed back up the stairs to the top of the wall.

Talon rushed over to the fallen knight, and Jakoby helped her up to a sitting position. She was barely breathing, and her face was badly burnt. "Long live the monarchy," she said with a raspy breath and died.

Jakoby's head sank to his chest. He said a quick prayer under his breath. "They're going to get wiped out by those demons of the air!" He stood and raised his sword. "But not if I can help it!" He ran for the stairs and headed to the top of the wall, his eyes blazing like fire.

From out of the smoking chaos, Crane rode up to them with his horse, Vixen, pulling his wagon. Hyrum sat on the bench beside him. "It's time to roll out. Everyone, get in."

Dyphestive rose. "I'm not going anywhere. The Monarchs need our help."

"We must go," Tatiana urged them. "Even we cannot overcome these forces. There are far too many dragons. Monarch City is lost. They wanted it this way."

"I don't care," Dyphestive said. "Running now wouldn't be right."

Crane reached into the back of the wagon and lifted the

war mace, Thunderash. "You'll need this!" He tossed it to Dyphestive, who snatched it out of the air with one hand and flipped it end over end. "What about the rest of you? The drawbridge is down. We can still escape the slaughter."

Grey Cloak stepped up beside his brother. "Where my brother stands, I stand." Streak crawled out of the back of the wagon and scurried toward him. Grey Cloak squatted down and picked up his dragon. "Streak!" Steak's pink tongue licked his face. "I missed you too." He let the dragon crawl over his shoulder and latch its claws into his back. He grimaced. "I don't like that."

"Listen to me," Tatiana said. "As much as I want to stand with you, we must flee. The Wizard Watch has foreseen doom for Monarch Castle. You must come with me. We are the keys to defeat Black Frost. You must trust me."

Dyphestive's eyes scanned the burning battlefield. He shook his head. "I can't stand by and watch it happen."

"You can't defeat them," Tatiana said as her eyes swept over the great dragons sweeping through the sky. "It's impossible."

Grey Cloak patted Streak's head and smirked. "We'll take our chances."

Tatiana's face fell.

"Grey Cloak, you take too many chances," Crane grumbled. "Don't make it a habit."

Hyrum stood up in the wagon. "Then you'll probably need this." He flung the Cloak of Legends to Grey Cloak.

Zora joined Grey Cloak, and he said, "Maybe you should go with Crane."

She shook her head. "I'm not going anywhere."

Reginald filled his hands with steel. "You know me, Tat." He spun his swords around in a blur of bright steel. "I hate to be insubordinate, but I never miss out on a fight."

A new wave of middling dragons flew overhead, carrying a netful of large stones. They opened their claws and released the net.

Stones plummeted to the ground like giant drops of rain.

Grey Cloak shouted, "Everyone take cover!"

45

Vixen lunged forward, jerking the wagon and almost knocking Crane over the back of his seat. Hyrum shot fire from his hands, blasting the falling hunks of stone to pieces. "Get this wagon out of here before it gets dashed to pieces!" Hyrum said.

Crane flicked his horse whip. Vixen sped out of the way along the wall.

The members of Talon dodged and dove to safety from the free-falling stones.

The foot soldiers spread across the courtyards were crushed under the weight of the large stones. The Honor Guards flattened themselves on the ground. Then on shaky legs, they stood up and shook their fists and shouted at the skies.

Another thunder of dragons flew by, and more stones

fell like rain. Bodies were crushed, and hearts stopped beating as the dead and wounded grew in number.

"We have to stop this," Grey Cloak said as he stood rooted, watching the skies above. The Riskers, poised in their dragon saddles, pulled back their bow strings and fired shots of mystically charged arrows that blew up their targets. He kept expecting the Sky Riders to swoop in at any moment. It didn't happen. "Where are they?"

"Where are who?" Zora asked as she huddled beside him.

"The Sky Riders," he said.

"Incoming!" Dyphestive hollered.

Another thunder of dragons rose up from the other side of the wall and released a netful of stone. The company dashed for cover under one of the bridges that traversed the gardens. They watched in horror as the ground troops were pummeled.

"How are we supposed to fight an enemy in the sky?" Razor asked. "They're cowards."

Zora tugged on Grey Cloak's arm. "Look," she said as she pointed at two men sneaking across the grounds. "It's Irsk and Finton. I'm getting my scarf back and killing them." She took off.

"No, wait," Grey Cloak said, but she slipped from his grasp. "Stay here. I'm going after her."

He lost sight of her in the dust billowing across the stone walkways. He dashed through the cloud, past a host of soldiers, and into a clearing. His eyes searched left and right. *There she is!*

Zora darted into a servant's entrance that led back inside the main castle and vanished.

He raced after her and into the servant's entrance leading into the kitchen. He ran right into Airius and stopped just before he plowed him over.

"You're supposed to be dead," Airius said with his snobbish tone and a horrified expression. "Why aren't you dead?"

"Because I wasn't finished with you yet," Grey Cloak said in a dark tone. He showed him his fist. "Where did the half-elf woman go?"

Airius jabbed his finger toward the front exit.

"You better hope I don't see you again, Airius. If I do, I'll feed you to the dragons." He ran after Zora and into the main hallway. Panic-stricken servants raced by.

He pushed past them, down the hall, peeking into chamber after chamber. He saw no sign of Zora or Irsk anywhere. He peeked up the stairs, stopped, looked, and listened. Nothing.

"Streak," he said out of desperate instinct. "Find Zora."

The runt dragon eased down Grey Cloak's body and onto the ground. His tongue flicked over the floor. With his nose to the ground, he moved like a bloodhound. He quickly made his way down the hall, making servants jump when he passed.

Grey Cloak followed. He wasn't sure how he knew Streak could hunt down Zora, but somehow he did. As they wound through the halls, he kept his eye out for danger. Aside from the servants, he didn't see anyone.

Where are all the Monarchs? They must be hiding somewhere, but I haven't seen any of them. He'd felt a strange gnawing in his gut ever since Tatiana had told him that the Monarchs had been warned. *How could they let this happen to their people? It doesn't make any sense. What are they trying to do, get themselves killed?*

Three Monarch Knights ran through one of the castle's intersections. The one in the rear caught a glimpse of Grey Cloak from the corner of his eye and stopped.

Grey Cloak hid behind a support column.

"Hold, men!" The knight that stopped drew his sword and fixed his eyes on Streak. "It's one of those demons from the sky."

The other two knights joined their comrade. The knights were imposing figures, regal and well-built. Their shining plate armor was fashioned to fit their large frames. Their open-faced helms were perfectly sculpted around their chiseled faces. They were all light-haired and light-skinned men. They brimmed with confidence.

Moving as one, they flanked Streak with their swords in hand. The one in the middle crouched. "Kill it."

46

Zora zeroed in on Irsk and Finton and never lost track of them. The sly pair navigated the castle passages like they'd been there a hundred times before. They moved quickly, slipping from her sight a couple of times, but she always caught back up.

You won't be getting away this time.

Irsk Mondo was nothing short of scum in her eyes. He preyed on innocent men, women, and children and sold them into slavery. Anyone who stood against him was beaten and killed. At least that was what Zora thought because many unruly prisoners had been made an example of and were taken away and never seen or heard from again.

Zora had spoken out against Irsk once. He'd back-handed her so hard it had knocked one of her back teeth out. His Iron Devils had used their fists to pummel the rest of her angry words out of her. But she still had anger, lots of it, and she was going to turn it loose on him.

She lost sight of the duo in a crowd of servants streaming down the halls. The women had their black dresses hiked up as they ran, and the men, with ladles and kitchen knives in their hands, hurried them along.

There they are.

The sinister pair slunk down a corridor, parted the huge set of iron double doors, and slipped inside. She peeked in after them.

Wooza.

There was no mistaking the chamber. It was Codd's crypt. A huge statue in beautiful armor stood in the middle, a giant shield in hand. No one guarded the chamber now, only the stone statues of Monarch Knights long past placed between the columns.

Finton Slay stepped up onto the huge pedestal, pulling his robes up over his ankles. He climbed up beside the statue and loosened Codd's stony grip on the shield. He muttered some mystic words, and the shield came free. He unstrapped the bracers for Codd's forearms and worked on the thigh and shin guards.

Those sacrilegious thieves.

With a quick look around the chamber, she saw no sign of Irsk Mondo, but another archway was open on the other side of the chamber. She slipped inside the crypt, her dagger in hand, and crept toward Finton Slay.

I'll take one then the other. I'll make them both pay.

The door closed behind her with an unseen force. She heard Irsk Mondo's laughter echoing all over the chamber.

Shades! He's using the Scarf of Shadows. Zora stabbed wildly near the door.

"Look at this. My wild butterfly has come to seek vengeance. How adorable," Irsk Mondo said.

Finton Slay turned to face her. His hands glowed with rose-colored fire.

"Zora, Zora, Zora, what in Gapoli were you thinking? Did you really hope to stop us?" Irsk asked.

"I don't hope to. I will."

Something hit her in the back so hard that she fell to all fours. It was followed by what felt like an invisible foot kicking her gut. Her dagger fell from her hand. She crawled after it. Her bare fingers stretched for the dagger and came within an inch. An invisible foot kicked it away.

The next thing she felt was a knee in her back, and an arm wrapped around her throat, choking her.

Irsk's lips touched her ear. "It looks like someone missed me. Too bad I didn't miss you. Pest!"

"Your breath is a pest!"

"Finish her off, and do it quickly," Finton said. "We don't have time for any more distractions."

Irsk jerked Zora off the floor. He pulled the scarf from

his face, and his lanky body appeared. "I give the orders, Finton. I'll hold her. You finish her. I don't like to get me nails dirty."

Finton approached with a cold look in his eyes. His hands brightened with mystic fire. "Hold still, woman. This won't hurt a bit."

47

Grey Cloak cleared his throat and stepped into full view. "Pardon me, honorable servants of the crown."

The three Monarch Knights turned their eyes toward him. "You're the man who hanged," the man in the middle said. "What sort of wizardry is this?"

Grey Cloak showed his open hands. "No wizardry involved. I assure you that I am alive and not a ghostly apparition." He glanced at Streak, who'd flattened on the ground and arched his neck to strike. "And that is my dragon. He's not in the brood of Riskers flying around. I swear to you that we're here to aid your cause."

"You were sentenced to death, and we shall carry that sentence out. I'll kill him. You kill the dragon," the leader said.

Grey Cloak rolled his eyes. "I don't have time for this. Smoke them, Streak!"

No sooner did he say it than smoke spewed from Streak's mouth. The knights backed away, fanning their faces and coughing. Grey Cloak and Streak dashed past them. The knights, renowned for their skill and instinct, chopped at them.

Streak squirted between their legs, and Grey Cloak jumped over a blade. He landed on one foot, but a knight grabbed his other ankle and yanked him hard to the ground.

"I have you!"

Grey Cloak kicked the knight in the nose but failed to break the man's grip.

All three of them pinned him to the smoke-covered ground. They landed hard punches with their metal gauntlets and kneed him in the ribs, attacking him like lions.

Time to change tactics before they break every bone in me. He might not have been as big as the strong men, but they were a lot slower in their armor. He poked two pairs of eyes with his fingers and twisted another man's helmet around his face. He jumped away only to have one of the knights snag his cloak and pull him down again. They piled on top of him, but all he could think of was saving his friend. *Zora!*

48

Doubled over in the clutches of Irsk Mondo, Zora made her move, which she'd been planning ever since they'd kidnapped her. They might have gotten the Scarf of Shadows, but they hadn't gotten her Ring of Mist. She'd squirreled it away and hid it whenever they'd searched her. She'd tucked the ring behind her knees, in her armpits, her hair, under her foot, wherever they weren't looking.

It had been her plan to use it when she saw a clear path to escape, but that had never happened. Now was her only chance. She fished the ring out of a small pocket in her pants and pushed it on her finger. She lifted her head and showed them the face of a defeated woman. "Go ahead. Do your best. Kill me. But I'll warn you. Talon will avenge me."

"No, they won't. They'll all be dead," Irsk said. He

nuzzled her cheek with his long chin. "But before you go, I would like to thank you for the scarf. It works admirably."

Finton spread the fingers of his burning hands and reached for her throat.

Zora curled her fist upward and rammed the ring right underneath Irsk's nose. The small metal flower opened its petals, and a fine mist sprayed out. Irsk Mondo's limbs turned to jelly. He dropped like a stone behind her.

Finton Slay's eyes burned red. His expression darkened into a snarl. "You won't escape me!"

A DAGGER FLASHED down at Grey Cloak's exposed chest. He grabbed the knight's wrist and pushed it back. "I'm on your side!"

All four men rolled and thrashed over the floor. Grey Cloak tried to squirm free, time and again, only to be reeled back into the knot of surging metal bodies.

The Monarch Knights earned their title that day. They were fierce and relentless.

Grey Cloak kicked one knight in the chin. The knight smiled in response through the smoke and licked the blood off his teeth. Grey Cloak popped the man under the chin a second time with his toe, and the knight cried out as he bit his tongue.

"Hold still, elf!" the leader said as he grabbed Grey Cloak by the ankles and held him fast. "We have you now!"

Another daunting figure appeared from the smoky hallway and punched the lead knight in the face with his massive fist. The knight dropped like a rock.

Grey Cloak bounced to his feet. "Dyphestive!"

Dyphestive locked arms with another knight, and they started headbutting one another. The knight still had his helmet on.

"Fool!" the knight said. "I'll crack your head open like an egg." They battered heads like rams butting horns. The knight's legs wobbled. He sank to the ground, muttering, "Impossible," and passed out.

Dyphestive, Tatiana, Razor, Jakoby, and Leena surrounded the last standing knight, who faced off with them, his longsword in two hands. His eyes were as big as saucers. "No matter. I'll finish all of you."

"No, you won't," Tatiana said. With a flick of her wrist, the knight flew upward into the ceiling. He hit his head and crashed back to the ground, knocked out cold.

Grey Cloak and Streak were off and running. "I have to find Zora."

Dyphestive hollered after him. "Grey Cloak, wait!"

FINTON SLAY LUNGED for Zora's throat with claw-like

burning fingers. He stumbled over the hem of his robes, fell, and struck his chin on the floor.

Zora bounced on his back with both feet and knocked the wind right out of the fragile man. The fire on his fingers went out. She reached for her dagger and clocked him in the back of the head with the pommel. The necromancer lay flat on the stones.

She moved to Irsk Mondo, removed the Scarf of Shadows from his neck, and put it on. Then she put her dagger against his throat. With her chest heaving, she said, "You're never going to hurt anyone ever again."

The doors to the crypt burst open.

Grey Cloak and Streak sped inside Codd's crypt. Zora had a dagger against Irsk's throat. "Zora, no," he said in a calm voice.

She sobbed. "He deserves it."

"I know. I know. But this is not the right way. Not in cold blood." He kneeled down beside her and gently removed the dagger from her grip.

Zora threw her arms around him and hugged him tight. "I hate him. I hate all of them."

"I know. It looks like you really gave it to them. I'm impressed."

She broke her embrace, wiping her eyes, and laughed. "Finton tripped and knocked himself out."

"Really?" Grey Cloak chuckled. "Wizards and their robes. You'd think they'd have learned to wear trousers by now."

"A cloak is little better," she said with a sniff.

"I'll never trip with this one. It's like a part of me." He covered her shoulders with his arm and led her toward the door. "We better move."

"What about them?"

"We'll tie them up and feed them to the dragons." He smirked. "How does that sound?"

"Good."

Dyphestive rushed into the room, leading the others. "Whew, you're okay!"

"Well enough." Grey Cloak searched his brother's eyes after Jakoby closed them inside. "What's going on?"

"It's the monarchy. They've raised the flags of surrender," Dyphestive said.

Grey Cloak couldn't hide his incredulity. "What? I thought the Monarchs never surrendered."

Jakoby spoke. "They don't." The dark-skinned knight was covered with half a dozen wounds. "Something isn't right. We must fight."

"We will fight," Dyphestive agreed. "We can't ever give in to Dark Mountain. What do we do, Grey Cloak?"

Grey Cloak scooped Streak into his arms. "We'll find a

way. We'll make the Riskers pay." He searched the faces of his friends and added, "Where's Than?"

WILL *Grey Cloak and Dyphestive achieve the impossible and save Monarch City?*

What happened to the mysterious otherworlder, Than?

PLEASE LEAVE A REVIEW OF MONARCH MADNESS. THEY ARE A HUGE HELP. LINK!

IT ALL UNRAVELS IN BATTLEGROUND: Dragon Wars - Book 7. On Sale Now at Amazon. US Purchase Link:

THE FIGURINE OF HEROES/HORRORS – In Book 6 you were introduced to a new character brought forth by Grey Cloak's use of the Figurine of Heroes, Selene. Selene originally appears in the Chronicles of Dragon – Series 1. If you've read the books, well, you know Selene's history quite well, and if you haven't, you might want to check them out. Oh, and Than, aka Nath Dragon, is from The Chronicles of Dragon as well. As I've said in many of my other books, all of my worlds will tie together, in one way or another. That's what makes fantasy fun!

Learn more about Than and Selene at:

The Hero, the Sword, and the Dragon – Book 1

Or

The Chronicles of Dragon Collection – Books 1-10

AND IF YOU haven't already, signup for my newsletter and grab 3 FREE books including the Dragon Wars Prequel. WWW.DRAGONWARSBOOKS.COM

TEACHERS AND STUDENTS, if you would like to order paperback copies for you library or classroom, email craig@thedarkslayer.com to receive a special discount.

GEAR UP in this Dragon Wars body armor enchanted with a +2 Coolness factor/+4 at Gaming Conventions. Sizes range from halfling (Small) to Ogre (XXL). LINK . www.society6.com

ABOUT THE AUTHOR

Craig Halloran resides with his family outside his hometown of Charleston, West Virginia. When he isn't entertaining mankind, he is seeking adventure, working out, or watching sports. To learn more about him, go to WWW.-DRAGONWARSBOOKS.COM.

*Check me out on Bookbub and follow: HalloranOn-BookBub

*I'd love it if you would subscribe to my mailing list: www.craighalloran.com

*On Facebook, you can find me at The Darkslayer Report or Craig Halloran.

*Twitter, Twitter, Twitter. I am there, too: www.twitter.com/CraigHalloran

*And of course, you can always email me at craig@thedarkslayer.com

See my book lists below!

ALSO BY CRAIG HALLORAN

Check out all my great stories...

Free Books

The Darkslayer: Brutal Beginnings

Nath Dragon—Quest for the Thunderstone

DRAGON WARS: PREQUEL

The Chronicles of Dragon Series 1 (10-book series)

The Hero, the Sword and the Dragons (Book 1)

Dragon Bones and Tombstones (Book 2)

Terror at the Temple (Book 3)

Clutch of the Cleric (Book 4)

Hunt for the Hero (Book 5)

Siege at the Settlements (Book 6)

Strife in the Sky (Book 7)

Fight and the Fury (Book 8)

War in the Winds (Book 9)

Finale (Book 10)

Boxset 1-5

Boxset 6-10

Collector's Edition 1-10

Tail of the Dragon, The Chronicles of Dragon, Series 2 (10-book series)

Tail of the Dragon #1

Claws of the Dragon #2

Battle of the Dragon #3

Eyes of the Dragon #4

Flight of the Dragon #5

Trial of the Dragon #6

Judgement of the Dragon #7

Wrath of the Dragon #8

Power of the Dragon #9

Hour of the Dragon #10

Boxset 1-5

Boxset 6-10

Collector's Edition 1-10

The Odyssey of Nath Dragon Series (New Series) (Prequel to Chronicles of Dragon)

Exiled

Enslaved

Deadly

Hunted

Strife

The Red Citadel and the Sorcerer's Power

The Darkslayer Series 1 (6-book series)
Wrath of the Royals (Book 1)

Blades in the Night (Book 2)

Underling Revenge (Book 3)

Danger and the Druid (Book 4)

Outrage in the Outlands (Book 5)

Chaos at the Castle (Book 6)

Boxset 1-3

Boxset 4-6

Omnibus 1-6

The Darkslayer: Bish and Bone, Series 2 (10-book series)
Bish and Bone (Book 1)

Black Blood (Book 2)

Red Death (Book 3)

Lethal Liaisons (Book 4)

Torment and Terror (Book 5)

Brigands and Badlands (Book 6)

War in the Wasteland (Book 7)

Slaughter in the Streets (Book 8)

Hunt of the Beast (Book 9)

The Battle for Bone (Book 10)

Boxset 1-5

Boxset 6-10

Bish and Bone Omnibus (Books 1-10)

CLASH OF HEROES: Nath Dragon meets The Darkslayer mini series

Book 1

Book 2

Book 3

The Henchmen Chronicles

The King's Henchmen

The King's Assassin

The King's Prisoner

The King's Conjurer

The King's Enemies

The King's Spies

The Gamma Earth Cycle

Escape from the Dominion

Flight from the Dominion

Prison of the Dominion

The Supernatural Bounty Hunter Files (10-book series)

Smoke Rising: Book 1

I Smell Smoke: Book 2

Where There's Smoke: Book 3

Smoke on the Water: Book 4

Smoke and Mirrors: Book 5

Up in Smoke: Book 6

Smoke Signals: Book 7

Holy Smoke: Book 8

Smoke Happens: Book 9

Smoke Out: Book 10

Boxset 1-5

Boxset 6-10

Collector's Edition 1-10

Zombie Impact Series

Zombie Day Care: Book 1

Zombie Rehab: Book 2

Zombie Warfare: Book 3

Boxset: Books 1-3